"How…how long have you been standing there?"

He came into the kitchen, a strange intensity on his face. Bella swallowed. The music segued to some slow, melancholic tune…*will you still love me tomorrow.…*

"Long enough," he said, his voice thick.

Her cheeks heated. She wanted to smile, say something casual, easy, but the look on his features stopped her.

"Long enough for what?" she whispered, thinking of his men in her room, going through her computer. The photo in her bag. Did he know? His gaze held hers. He came closer—very close. Bella reached behind her, bracing herself against the counter where she knew there was a knife. Even so, a dark carnal ribbon of desire unfurled inside her.

Dear Reader,

There's a reason fairy tales have been retold, rewritten and loved throughout the centuries—it's because they deal with basic ethical questions that affect all of us. And they do it by delightfully juxtaposing opposites like good versus evil, strange versus ordinary, appearance versus reality.

One of my favorite fairy tales as a child was *Beauty and the Beast,* the story of a handsome prince who is locked by a spell into the body of an ugly beast, and Beauty, who sees beneath the beast's exterior and falls in love.

I wanted to play with this trope—this deception of appearances—in the third installment of my Sahara Kings series. In this story, Sheik Tariq Al Arif has been badly damaged both physically and emotionally by his family's arch nemesis. He now hides in a dark, cold stone monastery on the cliffs of a remote windswept island. All the world believes he is dead. But not Bella DiCaprio. She believes there is more to the mysterious, scarred stranger who hides behind walls, and she's intent on exposing him. But Bella plays a game of deception herself. Will the truth destroy the love that grows between them, or will it be deadly?

I hope you enjoy Bella and Tariq's journey to their own happy ever after.

Loreth Anne White

LORETH
ANNE WHITE

Surgeon Sheik's Rescue

HARLEQUIN®
entertain, enrich, inspire™

Recycling programs
for this product may
not exist in your area.

ISBN-13: 978-0-373-27791-9

SURGEON SHEIK'S RESCUE

Books by Justine Davis

Harlequin Romantic Suspense

Silhouette Romantic Suspense

Other titles by this author available in ebook format.

LORETH ANNE WHITE

was born and raised in southern Africa, but now lives in Whistler, a ski resort in the moody British Columbia Coast Mountain range. It's a place of vast wilderness, larger-than-life characters, epic adventure and romance—the perfect place to escape reality. It's no wonder she was inspired to abandon a sixteen-year career as a journalist to escape into a world of romance fiction filled with dangerous men and adventurous women.

When she's not writing you will find her long-distance running, biking or skiing on the trails and generally trying to avoid the bears—albeit not very successfully. She calls this work, because it's when the best ideas come.

For a peek into her world visit her website, www.lorethannewhite.com. She'd love to hear from you.

For Patsy Adkins, and all readers like her—
you make it worthwhile. Thank you.

Chapter 1

The late February mist rolled in thick, tattered swaths off the Atlantic as Bella DiCaprio rode her bike along the exposed cliff tops of Ile-en-Mer, one of the tiny, storm-ravaged islands off the French coast of Brittany. Water poured from the brim of a red rain hat pulled low over her brow, snaking down the matching slicker Madame Dubois had loaned her for the duration of her employment as housekeeper. The old-fashioned bicycle was on loan, too, tires slipping in black mud as she negotiated a narrow trail through the heath.

Bella had been on the island two weeks now. She was using the name Amelie Chenard and she'd taken a job in the home of Estelle Dubois, a wealthy and eccentric widow who'd once worked in theater and been married to a Parisian banker.

The fact Bella was not in possession of a work visa did not faze the colorful Madame in the slightest—she was happy to pay in cash, under the table. More than a house-keeper, Estelle Dubois seemed to want someone to amuse her two pampered Papillons, particularly the youngest, a seven-month-old pup named Kiki. Part of Bella's job was to walk Kiki once a day, and play with her. The male dog was old and arthritic and preferred to spend his days sleeping in his basket by the fire.

The arrangement suited her fine. Now that she'd settled into a routine, Bella had plenty of free time for her *real* mission—to investigate the mysterious stranger who lived in an imposing stone abbey that loomed over cliffs on the bleak windward side of the island, accepting the brunt of the Atlantic storms.

Island lore claimed the foreboding structure—built in the high medieval period and renovated over the centuries—was haunted by the ghost of an abbess who'd been killed during a Breton revolt in the twelfth century. The abbess's headless body was said to have been walled behind rock in the dungeons, her head staked outside on the monastery gates as a warning to others who might shelter rebels.

Some said in a certain slant of moonlight the abbess's ghost could be seen floating through the arches. Others claimed they heard her screams when winter storms blew and fog swirled thick over the surrounding heath.

Whatever anyone wanted to make of it, the legend gave Bella an excuse to poke around. And, if she was right about who was living in that monastery now, she'd nail a journalistic scoop that would salvage her career, rock U.S. politics and put her name squarely back on the political news map.

If the story didn't kill her first.

Already, she'd been attacked by three men back home in Washington, D.C. If it hadn't been for the intervention of two cooks from a nearby Chinese restaurant, she was certain she'd be dead. She'd also been followed, her apartment ransacked and her hard drive hacked. Fearing for her life, Bella had fled the States and come in secret to this island. Fear was one of the reasons she was hiding under an assumed identity now, as she continued to track down her story.

Bella had gone looking for the Mont Noir Abbey during her first days on the island when the weather had been slightly more gracious. She'd found the black stone structure to be a startling mix of architectural periods, but predominantly gothic with spires and turrets reaching into the mist. Parts of it were still in ruin. The monastery had been constructed right at the cliff edge overlooking the Atlantic, a sharp plunge down to where waves pounded rocks far below. The extensive grounds were enclosed by an eight-foot-high stone wall topped with iron spikes. A sign in French warned trespassers to steer clear of the wrought-iron gates.

Bella had rung the bell at the gate, but no one answered.

Poking her telephoto lens through the bars she'd managed to capture some haunting architectural shots of the spires, arched windows, massive flying buttresses, gargoyles, but she'd suddenly noticed the security cameras atop the stone pillars flanking the gates tracking her motion. Then she'd detected more cameras positioned at discreet intervals between the spikes and creepers along the perimeter wall, and a frisson of unease ran through her.

Glancing slowly up, she caught sight of a dark figure in one of the mullioned windows in the upper floor window, watching her. But a shroud of mist sifted in from the sea, cloaking the abbey, and Bella had quickly returned to Madame's to serve the afternoon coffee.

Then just yesterday, while Bella had been in the village *boulangerie* buying fresh *pain au chocolat* for Madame, through the misted windowpanes of the little bakery she'd glimpsed a tall, dark figure moving down the cobbled sidewalk, his profile hidden by the hood of his black cape. Despite a limp, his stride was swift. Two dark-complexioned men in suits flanked him closely. Wind gusted, revealing a holster under the jacket of the man closest to the window.

Bella's pulse quickened and she spun round, trying to catch a glimpse of the hooded man's face. In the process she fumbled and dropped the small change being handed to her by the *boulangerie* owner who'd smiled at Bella's sudden distraction.

"He's the stranger from the other side of the island," the owner said as she helped Bella gather her coins.

"Do you know where he comes from?" she said, pocketing the change and picking up her basket of chocolate croissants.

The owner gave a Gallic shrug, pouting her lips. "Who knows?" She leaned forward, dropping her voice conspiratorially. "And we don't ask. Important people—rich, famous people—come to our island every summer. They come because we don't bother them. We don't try to guess who they are and we don't talk to paparazzi. But *their* estates lie on the southeast side of Ile-en-Mer where the climate is more temperate. Who would live on the west cliffs, and in winter? In a place that is haunted?" She gave a huff. "It's beyond me."

Bella thanked the owner and dashed out into the chill air. But the caped stranger was gone, the cobblestone streets eerily deserted.

"He goes by the name of Tahar Du Val," Madame told her in French that afternoon as Bella served the croissants and coffee, a fire crackling in the hearth, the little dogs curled in a fur ball in front of the flames. "You are very interested in this occupant of Abbaye Mont Noir, *non*—this dark man with his one eye and secrets?" Madame accepted the cup and saucer from Bella as she spoke, arthritis making her movements awkward.

"I'd love to visit his abbey, ask him about the ghost—research for my novel," she lied. "The more I know about him, the easier it'll be to approach him."

Madame took a sip of her coffee, her watery blue gaze fixed on Bella over the rim of her cup. And Bella reminded herself to be cautious—there was a sharp and analytical mind behind that papery skin, the powdery rouge, the red lipstick. Estelle Dubois could read people better than most.

"He moved into the abbey last August," Madame said, her features going slack and thoughtful as she dipped her croissant into the milky coffee. "He arrived with another man—"

Bella glanced up sharply. "What man?"

"I think he might have been Monsieur Du Val's brother," she said, delivering the soppy croissant to her mouth. "He was younger, a little broader in the shoulder, slightly shorter. And according to the villagers who saw his face—he and the monsieur have similar features."

Bella's pulse quickened, but she kept her expression neutral as she crouched down, opened the fire grate and poked at the logs. "Did he stay long?"

"Long enough to organize the employees at the abbey and see to the shipping-in of furniture," Madame said around her croissant. "And he handled the grocery shopping in the first weeks, before a chef came and took over."

"Did this man give a name?" Bella asked.

"*Non.* He barely spoke beyond what was necessary to do his business in the village."

Dryness tightened Bella's throat. Calmly, quietly, she reached for Madame's empty plate.

"Then one day, a private ferry came over from the mainland with gymnasium equipment," she said. "A woman came with it."

Bella stilled. "A dark-haired woman, exotic-looking?"

Madame's penciled brow rose quizzically. "No, the woman was fair. I think she had something to do with the gymnasium equipment, perhaps a personal trainer. But she left very abruptly, the next day—she was angry when she boarded the ferry."

"How do you know all this?"

"Jean-Claude, the ferryman who lives in the hut at the end of the pier. The younger man departed the island late September. He returned a few times until the end of November, but we haven't seen him since. And when all the summer visitors were gone and the winter storms started rolling in, that's when Monsieur Du Val started walking alone along the headland. Every day at precisely four-thirty. Always he wears his cape with the hood, and his black eye patch. His limp, it has been improving. After Christmas he began dining late every Tuesday night at Le Grotte below the hotel. He sits alone in a stone alcove in front of a window that overlooks the harbor. The maître d' draws the curtain across the alcove for privacy, and Monsieur Du Val's men sit close by at another table, watching the door. He orders a la carte and always a bottle of cabernet franc from the Chateau Luneau estate in the Loire Valley."

Bella knew the winery—it all fit.

It *had* to be him.

She stole a quick glance at the ornate Louis XVI clock on the mantel above the fire. Almost 3:30 p.m. "You're certain Monsieur Tahar walks along the cliffs at the same every day?" she said.

"*Oui*. Pierre, the sheep farmer on the other side, goes

to bring in his flock before dark. He sees the Monsieur in the distance, always at the same time."

"You talk to this farmer?"

"Everyone on this island talks, Amelie." She held up a gnarled finger in warning. "But always, the talk stays here, on the island. It has been this way for centuries."

The whole island felt liked it was locked in medieval time, thought Bella as her attention went back to the Louis XVI clock. Madame's eyes followed Bella's gaze and a smile curved along her mouth, red lipstick feathering deep into wrinkled creases.

"Go, Amelie," she said with a dismissive wave of her veined hand. "Go see him for yourself. All this talk has exhausted me. But feed the dogs first, and don't forget to lock the house when you go. Put the key under the mat so you don't wake me when you return."

Leaving Estelle Dubois nodding in front of the fire with her half-finished cup of milky coffee, Bella ran through drizzle to her separate maid's quarters across a small courtyard strung with a washing line and trellised with grapevines thick as her arm at the bases. Moss-covered clay pots fringed the whitewashed walls, the vegetation inside them brown and tangled by winter frost.

She shrugged into a warm sweater and jacket, then on second thought shucked the jacket in favor of the red rain slicker and matching hat. Even though weather on this leeward side of the island might be mild, rainstorms could be lashing the windward coast—she'd learned this fast enough. Over her thick socks she pulled on gum boots. Bella glanced in the mirror and gave a wry smile. She looked more like a mariner in a fish commercial than a seasoned political reporter. She grabbed the bike, wheeled it through the courtyard, and began to pedal up the twisting dirt road that led to the cliffs on the far side of the little island, camera bag slung across her chest, the cold air sinking deep into her lungs.

An hour later Bella stood atop the cliffs holding her bike and breathing hard as curtains of mist swirled and rain drove in squalls. Waves boomed unseen on rocks far below the sheer cliff drop. Light began to fade, and she felt a sharp drop in temperature. She began to shiver as dampness crawled into her bones.

Then suddenly, at four-thirty, just as Madame had said, a hooded, black figure in a swirling cloak materialized from the mist, walking along the headland, fading in and out of the shifting brume like a specter.

Bella laid her bike down on the heath, removed her camera from the bag.

Zooming in with her telephoto lens she watched him stop right at the cliff edge, his back to her. He pulled back his hood, revealing thick, shoulder-length hair, black as a raven's feathers. Face naked to the driving rain, he stared out to sea as if a sentinel watching for a lost ship, his cloak flapping at his calves.

Far below him waves crashed as the Atlantic heaved itself against the rock face, hurling icy spray up into the mist.

Something strange unfurled inside Bella.

He looked so alone, as if daring the elements to hurt him in some kind of bid for absolution. Yet in his shoulders there remained a subtle set of defiance.

Bella clicked off a few shots, zoomed in closer. Her lens was powerful, state-of-the-art. Her two-timing ex-boyfriend, Derek, had helped her choose the camera a mere two weeks before the newspaper budget cuts that saw Bella being laid off. The announcement she was being axed from the political news desk while the paper held on to the unionized deadwood had come as a gut-punching shock to Bella. One minute she was a respected, up-and-coming reporter covering the run-up to the presidential primaries and the bombing of the Al Arif royal jet at JFK. Then in the blink of an eye she was cast out on the street, unemployed, wondering how in hell she was going to make her next rent payment without cutting into her minimal severance payout.

Bella's job, her success, defined her. And her sudden unemployment cut to the heart of her insecurities and self-esteem that came with having been abandoned as a baby. It was something she'd never been able to shake.

Oh, she'd hunted for new work, but the tide had turned on print media. Papers were hurting. And there was a glut of journalists, just like her, pounding on doors.

In desperation Bella had resorted to writing a blog for a website called Watchdog—theoretically an internet news portal, but one that had been scathingly referred to as "that conspiracy theorist site." And because the blog gig was unpaid, she'd been forced to take housekeeping jobs to support her political writing "hobby." It was about as low as a political sciences and journalism graduate could go.

Derek, of course, had kept his photography job at the *Washington Daily,* courtesy of the boss's daughter. He'd informed Bella of his infidelity the same day as her layoff. Bella didn't know which had hit her harder.

She'd show them, she thought as she watched her target through her lens, fingers going numb from cold, her teeth starting to chatter. This man was going to be her route back.

But she had to be careful. She still didn't know who had tried to kill her back home, or why. Or how this man from the abbey—the subject of her investigation—might

be linked to Senator Sam Etherington, the man likely to
be voted next U.S. president come the November election.

Bella willed him to turn around now, show his face. Instead, he began to move farther along the cliff, making his
way toward a narrow, black headland that jutted out into
the sea. Bella left her bicycle lying in the heather and followed him on foot, at a distance. The mist grew thicker,
the light dimmer, the air even cooler.

Right at the very tip of the headland, he stopped again.
A ship's horn boomed out at sea and through the mist came
the faint, periodic pulse of a lighthouse unable to penetrate
the thickening darkness and fog.

She snapped a few more frames, then stilled as he
moved even closer to the edge. He stood there, as if daring gravity to take him over, suck him down into the crashing sea. She was reminded suddenly of a similar cliff,
Beachy Head in England, where the suicide rate was sur-
passed only by the Golden Gate Bridge in San Francisco,
and where the *Beachy Head* Chaplaincy Team conducted
regular patrols in an attempt to spot—and stop—potential
jumpers. This was a similar cliff. No patrols. Just her ob-
serving him in the darkening gloom. A chill chased over
Bella's skin. She lowered her camera, half poised to run,
stop him, help him. But he remained still as a statue, coat
billowing out behind him, his hair now slick with rain.

Slowly she raised her camera back to her eye, the shut-
ter *click, click, clicking* as she struggled to tamp down a
mounting rush of apprehension. Bella readjusted her telephoto lens, zooming in as close as she could go. But as
she was about to press the button, he turned suddenly to
face her.

She sucked in her breath.

For a nanosecond she was unable to move, think.

He stared at her with his good eye, black as coal. An

eye patch covered his left eye and the left side of his face was marred by a violent scar that hooked from temple to jaw, drawing the left side of his mouth down into a permanent, sinister scowl. But the hawkish, arresting features, the aquiline nose, the arched brows—they were burned into her memory after staring at so many photos of him before the explosion.

It was him.

Sheik Tariq Al Arif, the famed neurosurgeon, next in line to the throne of Al Na'Jar—supposedly dead from injuries sustained by a terrorist bomb blast at JFK Airport in New York last June—was *alive.* And she'd found him. Living in a cold, haunted abbey in France.

Emotion flooded her chest as she clicked off a rapid succession of shots of his face. She had her story. It was right here. At least part of it. This was the beginning, the tip of the iceberg that could sink Sam Etherington's bid for the White House—if she could just understand the rest.

He glared at her as she shot off her frames, utterly still, his face wet with rain, everything in his posture warning her not to dare take a step toward him. And suddenly, as her pulse calmed a little, Bella saw not only hostility in his features, but pain.

Slowly she lowered her camera, ashamed of her own hunger to expose him.

Fog thickened around him, turning him to a shadowy phantom and she realized with a start it would be fully dark any minute. She needed to find the path through the heather, back to her bike, make her way back down the cliff before nightfall. But she hesitated—what about him?

Did he walk back to that monastery, alone, in pitch blackness, so close to the treacherous cliff edge? Worry sparked through her.

Then, almost imperceptibly, he seemed to move toward

her. At first Bella thought it was a trick of the mist, then a spark of fear shot through her—how far would he actually go to keep his secret?

How far would his powerful family go?

The memory of her attack curled through her mind, and fear fisted in her chest.

She was all alone here. If her body was found smashed and broken in waves below the cliff, it would be deemed an accident, blamed on the weather, a foolish young American caught by fog and nightfall too close to the edge.

Bella started backing away, then she turned and hurried along the path to where her bicycle lay on its side in the heather.

Picking up her bike, the chrome wet and icy in her hands, she glanced back over her shoulder, but he was gone—a ghost dissolved into mist.

Tariq stormed into the hall of his abbey, wind swirling in behind him as the great wooden doors swung shut. Fat white candles flickered in sconces along the stone wall and a dark, hot energy rolled through him.

"That woman from the village—" he barked loudly to his men in Arabic "—the one poking around the gates, taking photos of the abbey. I want to know who she is, where she comes from, what she wants with me, and then I want her gone!"

He shrugged out of his drenched cape, slung it over a high-backed chair and strode through the dark halls to his library where a fire crackled in the stone hearth, shutting the door behind him.

His library was the one room in this stone monstrosity that he preferred to inhabit. A smaller office with his desk and papers lay off it. The rest of abbey remained unlit and cold, some of it still partially in ruin, wind whistling through cracks and moaning up in the turrets like the ghost of the abbess herself. Haunted suited him fine—he was a mere ghost of himself anyway, a broken shadow, not living, not dead.

Irritably, Tariq plucked a leather-bound copy of a book by Algerian-French writer and absurdist philosopher Albert Camus from the shelves. He settled into his chair by the fire, flipped it open.

But he couldn't concentrate.

He put on Mischa Maisky's rendition of the prelude from Bach's Cello Suite no. 1. It always soothed him. It reminded him of Julie. Of life, of power, of beautiful times.

He leaned his head back in his chair, arms flopping loosely over the armrests. The first notes of the cello washed over him. And as the music rose in crescendo, Tariq closed his eye, imagining his own fingers moving on the strings, the Pernambuco bow in his hand, the solid shape of the finely carved instrument between his knees. Whenever he'd played this piece, his whole world seemed to drop away, leaving only the moment as the harmony filled him, breathed into him, became part of him. He let his chest rise and fall to the rhythm....

But then he saw *her* eyes, bright like spring crocuses, staring at him through the misted *boulangerie* window, her dark curls tousled about her pale, heart-shaped face like some untamed thing. Tariq cursed, shutting out the image. Another flowed into his mind as the music rose—the sight of her on the heath, like a mythical Red Riding Hood, drifting in and out of curtains of fog as she followed him with her camera. He tried to block her out again.

She was too bright.

It was like shutting your eyes after staring at a lamp— the afterimage burned on your retinas.

Tariq lurched to his feet, strode to where his cello rested

in a stand against the wall. With the fingertips of his right hand he caressed the sleek curves of finely grained Balkan maple, a wood of resilience and excellent tone. A cold heaviness pressed into his heart. Never again would he play this exquisitely crafted instrument. Never again would he operate. His left hand was his dominant one, and it was his left side that had been forever crippled in the series of blasts that had killed his fiancée. It had been an attack on his country, on him.

He should have been the one to die. Not her.

This war was against *his* family, not Julie. Falling in love with her, bringing her into the Al Arif enclave, had made her a target. And he, a doctor—a surgeon—had been unable to save her at the critical moment.

Julie's death was his fault.

The Moor, the as yet faceless archenemy of the Al Arif dynasty, had stolen everything that mattered to Tariq, everything that had defined him, everything that made life worth living, leaving him nothing but a coarse lump of a man, an empty, cold shell who'd failed the only woman he'd ever loved. Self-hatred fisted in Tariq's chest. His gaze was slowly, inexorably, pulled toward the floor-to-ceiling gilt mirror on the wall.

He was sickened by what he saw in that mirror. Sickened by what he'd become, inside and out. Crippled, broken. Bitter. Twisted.

That prying young woman in the red coat had pierced through the numb rhythm of his life on the island. She'd reawakened his pain. She'd gone and reminded him a world lurked out there beyond these cold stone walls—a world inhabited by a dangerous enemy who could *still* hurt his family and the people of his desert kingdom.

She'd made him look into that mirror—and he hated her for it.

With his right hand, Tariq snatched a bronze paper-weight off the side table and hurled it across the room with all his might. It crashed into the mirror, shattering glass outward in a starburst. Shards tinkled softly to the Persian rug along with the dull thud of the paperweight.

Anger coiled in his stomach as Tariq stared at the broken glass, shimmering with light from the flames. All he had left was his privacy, the numbness of grief.

Whatever she wanted, he was not going to allow her to take *that* from him. Tariq was going to get his men to find out who she was, what she wanted, then he'd take action to ensure she stayed the hell away from him and his abbey.

Chapter 2

Bella yanked off her muddy gum boots, flicked on the lamp, closed the drapes. She shrugged out of her wet coat and hat, shook out her hair and pulled on her favorite thick, soft sweater.

Turning up the oil heater, she powered her laptop, connected her camera and began to download the photos she'd taken. Edgy with adrenaline, she paced her small room as she waited for the high-resolution images to load. The wind grew stronger outside, rattling at her windows, seeking its way in through ancient cracks. Rain began to tick against the panes.

Bella drew her sweater closer, rubbing her arms as she willed the heater to warm faster. Before her termination with the *Washington Daily,* the two key stories she'd been following were Senator Sam Etherington's bid for his party nomination for president, and the terrorist bombing of the Al Arif royal jet at JFK.

Etherington had since won his party's endorsement and was now considered to be a shoo-in for president, unless he badly misstepped between now and November. The Al Arif bombing story Bella had scored by default.

She'd been with her then-boyfriend, Derek, on a separate assignment at JFK when the blast occurred. They'd seized the moment, covering the event from an eyewitness perspective, and the *Daily* had let Bella run with the story as it continued to unfold over the following days, weeks, months.

She'd done good work—demonstrating a talent not only for political reporting but showing her capability as a passionate features writer, digging deep into the characters and issues behind the tragedy.

Derek in turn had shot what was now an iconic image of the injured and bloodied Dr. Tariq Al Arif racing from the burning jet with his fiancée, Julie Belard, hanging limp in his arms.

Seconds after Derek had taken that famous photo, the prince had dropped to his knees and tried to resuscitate Julie, but a second blast caused by escaping jet fuel had sent chunks of shrapnel flying into the back of his head and left side of his body, severely wounding and concussing him. In the ambulance the sheik lapsed into coma. Days later he was flown home by his family where he was cared for in a private clinic. Seven weeks after the bombing, the palace press office put out a terse statement announcing Dr. Al Arif's death.

There were still no arrests, and there'd been no public memorial service—only a small private affair in Al Na'Jar attended by Tariq's immediate family. None of Julie Belard's family attended, which Bella had found strange.

The story seemed to end there, as had her job with the *Daily.*

But Bella had trouble letting go of both her job and the prince.

During the months of covering his story, she'd become obsessed with Tariq—the aggressively good-looking surgeon prince with a brilliant mind was also an accomplished cellist and fierce polo player. Horsemanship, she'd learned, was a talent Tariq had acquired as a young boy in his desert kingdom under the tutelage of his father. Music was a gift he'd inherited from his mother's side. But he'd also been a healer at heart, and this passion had led him into neurosurgery, and to the United States.

Bella had come to see Tariq as a man with one foot in an ancient and exotic past, the other firmly planted in a new world, and when she'd heard of his "death," something inside her had grieved.

Many a lonely night she'd spent staring at the photo of Tariq fleeing that jet, thinking of the anguish in his features, the desperate passion with which he'd tried to revive his fiancée. She realized, on some level, she'd fallen in love with the idea of the prince. This was why she was so unwilling to let go of him, or his story. It also felt unfinished.

And so it had started.

Desperate for a way to keep her hand in the political news scene, to finish what she'd started, Bella had taken a hotel housekeeping job and gone over to the "dark side" to join Watchdog. The site was run by Hurley Barnes, an old friend of Bella's from her college days, along with his techie girlfriend, Agnes, and their ex-CIA hacker buddy, Scoob.

It was ironically fitting, she supposed, for Bella Di-Caprio, an orphan—a reject who'd been abandoned as a two-day-old baby in a bassinet at a Chicago hospital facility for unwed mothers—to go live along the cyber fringes of society, writing with a bunch of wack-job-genius nerds, always struggling to be accepted by the mainstream but never quite managing to hang in, or pull it off.

Still, it grated—it went against everything she'd fought for her whole life—to be accepted. And her goal remained to get back, get even, prove that Bella DiCaprio was not done.

Not without a fight.

Bella's first order of blogging business for Watchdog had been to phone Julie Belard's father—Pierre Belard—France's ex-ambassador to the U.S. She'd wanted to interview him about the death of his daughter and her fiancé. The ambassador had explained that Tariq's funeral had been kept small for security reasons, and the Belards had understood the Al Arifs' need for privacy at this time. This was why they'd not attended.

When she asked the ambassador more about Julie as a person, he told Bella his daughter used to love to holiday with the extended Belard family on Ile-en-Mer off the Brittany coast, and as a child she'd been fascinated by stories of the ghost in the abbey on the far side of the island. He'd also said that for the past three years Julie had returned to Ile-en-Mer with Tariq to attend the opera festival held each summer on the island, and that the couple had gotten engaged there.

Bella had done more digging and discovered that a large financial donation had been made to the Ile-en-Mer opera fund in Julie's memory. After deeper cyber investigation with the help of her techie friend Scoob, Bella learned the donation had been made by a shell company owned by the Al Arif Corporation—the same company that had quietly purchased the Abbaye Mont Noir itself two years ago. Bella found it strange the donation had been made only in Julie's name.

Then, when she'd called an island travel agent inquiring

about the Abbaye Mont Noir and its ghost, the agent told her the new owner himself had recently moved in, and the abbey grounds had been closed off to the public. On probing further, Bella was told the owner was a mysterious and reclusive foreigner who'd been badly scarred down his left side. She'd become convinced it was Tariq living in that abbey, that the palace had lied about his death.

Her laptop beeped suddenly, jolting her back to the present—her download was complete.

Reseating herself at her computer, she hurriedly scanned the thumbnails for the shot where "Tahar" had turned his face to her. She clicked on it.

His mist-framed features mushroomed onto her screen, and Bella's heart started to pound. The intensity in his damaged features—the anguish, the pain, the rage—she'd captured it all in this haunting, ghostly image. And with his hood back off his head, his hair wet, she'd caught him somehow naked, stripped in the face of the elements. As raw and vulnerable as he once was powerful.

A strange energy curled through Bella.

She touched the screen with her fingertips, traced the lines of his face.

Why are you hiding?

What would it mean to you to be exposed?

She knew what it would mean to *her*.

It would be her way back into a *real* job, especially if she found out how this story linked to an anonymous tip she'd received alleging that Senator Sam Etherington had been behind an attempt to assassinate Tariq's youngest brother, Omair, in Algiers last summer.

The tip had been sent to Bella's Watchdog account after the Maghreb Moors—or MagMo—a terrorist group led by a mysterious man known only as The Moor, claimed responsibility for assassinating Tariq with the jet bomb.

Bella had run this news coupled with a hard-hitting blog post taking Senator Etherington to task on his national security stance, and asking how he could promise an electorate oil from a Al Na'Jar when the kingdom itself was under threat of a MagMo-fueled coup.

An anonymous instant message had popped up on her screen less than an hour after she hit Publish. It read:

You want to know the connection between Etherington and the Al Arifs? Etherington was behind a U.S. black ops unit attempt to assassinate Tariq's brother Omair in Algiers last summer. The unit is called STRIKE. Strategic Alliances, a D.C. consulting company, is the front for STRIKE. Just ask Travis Johnson who ordered him to have Omair killed... Oh, wait, you can't ask Johnson—coz he's dead himself!!!

The IM had exploded into an emoticon bomb puffing smoke. Another laughing face emoticon rolled next to the bomb.

Watchdog had tried to trace the IM, but whoever sent it was good, too good. Scoob laid a digital trap in the hopes of snaring the sender if another tip came in.

Meanwhile, Bella had tried to find out more about Strategic Alliances. All she'd learned was that the company consulted for the government, that the CEO was a man named Benjamin Raber, and that Travis Johnson, an employee under Raber, had been shot dead execution-style in an underground parking garage a month ago—no arrests, no leads. Nothing.

Scoob had helped her scour cyberspace for other links between the Al Arif family and Etherington, coming up only with a newspaper photo of Sam Etherington's missing ex-wife, Dr. Alexis Etherington. She'd been seen with Dr. Tariq Al Arif at a medical convention in Chicago more than ten years ago. The coincidence was strange.

No one ever found out what had happened to Alexis, an ophthalmic surgeon who, oddly, had been a specialist in the same genetic illness that had rendered Tariq's oldest brother, King Zakir, blind during the first year of his reign.

Blood humming, Bella had instantly called the palace press office in an attempt to locate Sheik Omair Al Arif, but the palace shut her down the minute they found she no longer worked for the *Daily*. It just fired her anger and lust to get this story. Bella continued searching for any online mention of Sheik Omair Al Arif, but he'd not made any public appearance for well over a year. He seemed to have simply vanished off the face of the earth.

Until, possibly, now.

Madame's words crawled through her mind.

I think the man might have been Monsieur Du Val's younger brother...according to the villagers who saw his face—he and the Monsieur have similar features...

Bella opened an older file on her laptop and pulled up Derek's iconic image of Tariq racing from the plane. In the photo the left side of his face was gashed open, awash with blood that filled his eye socket and blackened his torn, white shirt. His features were twisted with indescribable anguish.

She juxtaposed this image with the one she'd just taken on the cliff.

And there was no doubt in her mind.

It was him.

Tahar Du Val was Tariq Al Arif, next in line of succession to the Al Arif throne of Al Na'Jar.

The weight of her discovery suddenly felt heavy, a little frightening. Would exposing him bring danger to his door, or to hers? How did all this connect to Sam Etherington? And who had tried to kill her?

Outside the wind began to moan through the eaves, the wash line clinking against a pole in the courtyard.

Bella scrubbed her fingers through her curls, Madame Dubois's words sifting into her mind.

He started dining late every Tuesday night, at Le Grotte...always, he orders a bottle of cabernet franc from the Chateau Luneau estate in the Loire Valley...

Chateau Luneau was the winery owned by the Belard family.

She shut down her computer thinking she wasn't ready to post anything on her blog. Not yet. She wanted— needed—proof. And she wanted the *whole* story.

Tomorrow was Tuesday. Bella would be at Le Grotte tomorrow night, waiting for Tariq.

And come hell or high water, she was going to find a way to talk to him.

It was 10:45 p.m. when Bella entered the small restaurant above the ancient harbor. On further investigation, she'd been told that Tahar came to dine at Le Grotte at 11:00 p.m. each Tuesday, when the establishment was quietest.

The restaurant was constructed of stone, like most buildings in the medieval village. Leading off the tiny entranceway Bella could see an intimate dining area with white linen tablecloths and candles flickering in jars. A hostess stepped forward to take Bella's coat.

Shrugging out of her red slicker and hat, Bella tousled her fingers through her damp hair while making small talk about the weather. But inside she was wire-tense. It could be make or break tonight—move in on Tariq too fast, and she could lose all opportunity to talk to him.

The hostess showed Bella into the dining area. Her attention was immediately snagged by a small, stone-walled alcove with red curtain tied to the side. A table in the alcove was set for one, with a lone high-back chair facing the arched window that looked out over the harbor. But there was little to see outside tonight—fog pressed thick against the glass, moving, shifting, like a sentient thing seeking its way in.

He sits alone in a stone alcove in front of a window that overlooks the harbor. The maître d' draws the curtain across the alcove for privacy...

Anxiety fisted in her stomach, and a strange chill washed over her skin. Bella rubbed her arms as a maître d' with a startling waxed mustache scurried toward Bella. He reminded her of Agatha Christie's Hercule Poirot, which eased some of the tension. He thrust his hand out toward a table near the dimly lit bar, but Bella asked instead for the table nearest the alcove.

The maître d' frowned.

"The light is better here," Bella explained. "I've brought reading material and want to make notes." She paused. "And the place seems pretty empty tonight."

Grudgingly the maître d' pulled out the chair for her near the alcove. He set a wine list on the table, but his attention kept flicking back and forth between her and the door. Trepidation rose once again in Bella. She followed his glance to the door. It was almost 11:00 p.m.

Without looking at the wine list, Bella asked for a bottle of Chateau Luneau cabernet franc and a glass of water. Her intent was to have the bottle on her table and the label visible when Tariq arrived. She hoped to strike up a conversation about the winery, which could possibly lead to mention of the Belard family.

At the very least, she wanted to walk away tonight with an invitation to tour his abbey. She'd figure out how to play the rest as she went.

The wine might be a risky move, but Bella reminded herself that if she genuinely was Amelie Chenard, doing research for a gothic novel set in an old abbey on this island, trying to use the wine as a conversation opener with the abbey owner should not be suspicious in the slightest. After all, her employer had told her it was Tahar's favored choice. And Amelie had made no secret out of the fact she was seeking an invite to the abbey.

Nose clearly out of joint, the mustachioed maître d' bustled off to fetch the wine.

Bella turned her attention to the only other patrons in the establishment—a couple, maybe in their forties, were speaking intimately over a table in the far corner of the room. A bottle of champagne sweated in a silver bucket at their side and they were holding hands over the table. *Celebrating,* thought Bella. A wedding anniversary perhaps. Derek came suddenly to mind and a pang of remorse twisted through her. She really had thought he was different from the others. Was she that bad a judge of character when it came to men? Every relationship she'd ever entered had been very physical, had peaked fast, then crashed and burned. Sometimes she wondered if she was sabotaging her own efforts to be happy, as if choosing the wrong men was a way of avoiding commitment.

She needed to go slow next time, if there ever were a next time. After all, this story had already killed people and put her life at risk. But that also told her it was worth pursuing—and Bella never gave up without a fight.

The maître d' returned with the bottle and made a great show of holding the label out for her approval—Poirot was clearly going to be sommelier, maître d' and server rolled in one tonight.

Bella smiled, nodded, and he poured for her to taste. She sipped, and liked it a lot. While Poirot filled her glass she opened the menu, paling suddenly at the prices. The wine alone was going to kill her budget. Bella ordered the house salad, the cheapest item.

The maître d' sniffed at her choice. As he scuttled off, she removed her notebook and pen, along with a travel magazine, which she set upon the table at her side. A photo of an old castle graced the cover, and the magazine's top feature was an article on haunted properties down the coast of France. If the wine didn't spark conversation, the magazine might provide an opportunity to lead into a discussion about Abbaye Mont Noir and its ghost.

Angling her chair slightly for a clear view of both the entrance and the alcove where she expected Tariq to sit, Bella reached for her wineglass. But as she was about to take a sip, the restaurant door swung open, letting in a blast of blustery air that made the candles on the tables flicker wildly.

She froze, attention riveted on the door.

A giant of a man with Mediterranean complexion, hooked nose, dark eyes, expensive suit, entered the hallway. He paused, scanning the dining area. His eyes settled instantly on Bella.

Holding her gaze, he stepped sideways. Tariq entered beside him. He pushed back the hood of his cape, exposing his oil-black hair, the eye patch, the violence down the left side of his face. His bodyguard bent down, whispered something. Tariq's gaze shot to Bella.

His shoulders stiffened.

Bella felt her cheeks heat as she met the sheik's piercing gaze. The power of his stare was disconcerting. So was the way his scar pulled the side of his mouth into an inflexible sneer. She wondered in that moment why he hadn't opted for plastic surgery. Perhaps he didn't care.

It wasn't that his injuries made him unattractive—there

was something darkly mesmerizing about him. And his air of command, of presence, was instantly tangible, powerful. But the piratical eye patch, the angry scars, the downturned eye and mouth—it made him look dangerous, formidable. Almost a little otherworldly. Something dark and hot pumped into her blood.

Bella tried to swallow against the growing dryness in her mouth, her pulse now fluttering like a moth caught in a jar. She tried to offer a smile, but was unable to command her mouth to do so. Slowly, she lowered her glass, setting it on the table. Her hand was shaking slightly.

The energy in the room shifted. The couple in the far corner felt it, glancing sharply up from their candlelight tête-à-tête, and the maître d' rushed forward.

A second bodyguard entered behind Tariq. But as the hostess reached forward to take Tariq's cloak, he raised his palm, halting her.

"Good evening, Monsieur Du Val," the mustachioed maître d' intoned loudly as he approached Tariq. "Can we show you to your table?" He held his arm out in the direction of the waiting alcove.

Tariq said something quietly to the maître d', his eyes still fixed on Bella as he spoke. He then turned toward the door and drew the hood back up over his head.

Panic rose in her chest. He was leaving because of her! He'd taken one look at her sitting too close to his private table and he'd drawn his line in the sand.

The maître d' shot her an angry scowl as Tariq's bodyguard reopened the door and ushered the sheik out.

Tongues of panic licked fiercer. She couldn't, *wouldn't* let him leave. Not without talking to him, trying to explain why she'd tried to ambush him. Because this might be her one and only shot at approaching him, and it was blowing up in front of her eyes.

* * *

The restaurant door swung shut behind him. Tariq sucked the icy winter air deep into his lungs, trying to calm himself. Rain was turning to snow, fat flakes separating from diaphanous mist, wafting to the ground and winking out on the slick cobblestones at his feet. He strode up the street to his waiting limousine, focusing fiercely on controlling his limp, his visible weaknesses.

He should never have started coming into the village, or dining at the restaurant. Why he'd done it he wasn't sure. Maybe there was a distant need still buried somewhere deep inside him, a need for human connection.

But he had not anticipated the fierce lust that had gut-punched him at the sight of that woman in the restaurant. Tariq's hands fisted. Seeing her in that figure-hugging, black jersey dress, knee-high boots, long legs, her mass of dark curls giving her that just-risen-from-bed allure… it reminded him he was not a cold, numb ghost of a man at all. Rather, he was a disfigured, damaged, sorry echo of what he'd once been, with all the old needs still pumping hot and hungry in his blood.

His mind went to her face, so pale against the black liner she'd applied around her huge crocus-colored eyes. Eyes like an oasis. Something he wanted to drown himself in. And not once had her steady gaze left his.

She'd been sitting too close to his alcove in a restaurant that was basically empty. And he'd not failed to notice the distinctive label on the bottle of wine near her fine-boned hand, either. Chateau Luneau cabernet franc—the same wine he ordered every Tuesday night. The wine that came from the Loire Valley estate that had been in Julie's family for centuries.

His pulse quickened as he neared his vehicle. The startling fist of arousal that had slammed into him at the sight of her disturbed Tariq, as did the accompanying rush of adrenaline. He did not want to feel. Anything.

A cold anger calcified around his heart as he reached his limo, his guard stepping forward to open the door.

She'd positioned herself to ambush him. And Tariq knew why, at least on the surface. His men had done their digging.

She was Estelle Dubois's new housekeeper and dog sitter. She was also an author. Her name was Amelie Chenard. She came from the States, spoke good French, and had told Estelle Dubois that her great-grandmother's family hailed from this region. She was supposedly writing a gothic novel set on Ile-en-Mer, featuring the abbey and its ghost. And she wanted a tour of his estate.

She also did not have a work visa, had little money. Gossip around town had it that Madame Dubois was paying her under the table, which was not unusual for Madame, apparently. The old woman marched to her own drum, and always had.

On the surface Amelie Chenard's story seemed feasible, thought Tariq as he got in the limo, but he trusted nothing. And no one.

The limousine had been Omair's idea. Hide in plain sight, his brother had said. Make the image fit. He could hear Omair's words now.

The more important and mysterious you seem, the more these islanders will respect your privacy and keep their distance. The less likely they'll be to discuss you with outsiders.

Omair had been right about the islanders. Amelie Chenard was another story.

Suspicion snaked deeper into him.

Know your enemy. Keep him close.

Those had always been his father's words.

Tariq inhaled deeply as he leaned back into the limo seat. Again his brother Omair's words sifted to mind.

Tell me at once if anything unusual happens…our family, our country, our kingdom is at stake.

This was not just about him. Tariq's secret was also his family's secret. If Amelie Chenard was after something more than the abbey ghost… Bitterness filled his mouth and he cursed. He needed to face her, deal with, then dispose of her if necessary.

As his bodyguard climbed into the car he said, "Go tell that woman to be at the abbey tomorrow, 5:00 p.m. sharp. I'll see her then."

His man looked at him, a brief hesitation crossing his face.

"Now!" Tariq snapped.

If she gave him cause to suspect her motivation further, he'd ask Omair and his military intelligence team to investigate her. She'd be sorry she ever came prying.

Bella pushed through the restaurant's heavy wood door and rushed out into the frigid night. Frantically scanning the street, she saw his vehicle parked a short way up the hill, exhaust smoke beginning to puff white into the cold air, one of the doors still open. She began to run toward the car, aiming to apologize, explain, anything that might stop him from leaving, stop him from shutting her out permanently. She'd come so far for this story already, she would not let it die here in this cold cobblestone street.

But as she ran, a man suddenly appeared out from the shadow at her side, his huge form blocking the pale light from the streetlamp.

Bella froze, her mind hurtling back to the attack in D.C. She spun around to flee. But the man lurched forward and grabbed her arm in a viselike grip. She bit back the scream rising in her chest as the lamplight caught the man's face and she registered the raw-boned, dark features of the second bodyguard.

Air whooshed out of her.

"What in hell do you think you're doing!" she hissed, jerking her arm free, heart thumping loudly against her rib cage.

"Monsieur Du Val wanted me to inform you that if you wish to see him he will be available at the abbey tomorrow at 5:00 p.m." The man spoke French with the rolling *r*'s of Arabic and his right hand hovered close to his hip where Bella had seen a gun the other day.

Her gaze flashed to the waiting limousine. "He said *what?*" She wasn't sure she'd heard right.

"Report to the security gate at five, ring the bell, and someone will bring you in."

Before she could open her mouth again, the man turned and strode up to the waiting limo.

Incredulous, Bella stood rooted to the spot, watching him climb in. She heard the door slam. The vehicle pulled out into the narrow street. Brake lights flared bright at the top of the hill. The limo rounded the corner, then disappeared.

Silence pressed down.

Snowflakes wafted thicker around her and Bella began to shiver. The fog was coming up from the harbor dense and damp. She made her way back to the restaurant, feeling like an Alice who'd slipped into some strange alternate reality, because nothing felt real. But at least now she had her invite, if she could call it that.

Tariq leaned back in the dark interior of his vehicle as they headed up toward the deserted windswept side of the island. Snow was coming down very heavily at the higher elevation, blowing vertically. The wipers struggled to clear arcs across the windshield.

"What did she say?" he said quietly to his bodyguard in Arabic. "Is she coming?"

"I believe so."

Tariq closed his eyes, his tension increasing as they neared the spiked iron gates of the monastery.

This was his lair, his private home. He'd been forced to invite her inside, simply to ensure she was not a threat. Or was that all? Was there perhaps, buried deep down inside, a darker, more carnal part of himself that actually *wanted* to see her again, speak to her, maybe even touch her, satisfy a curiosity that went beyond the cerebral, or practical?

The irony twisted through him, along with a stab of trepidation.

Tariq had always been a physical man. A love and appreciation of women had always burned fierce and pure in his gut. But unlike his younger brother, he'd always been a one-woman man.

And for the last five years of his life, that one woman had been Julie. And her memory was still sharp.

An interest in someone else was not a transition Tariq was ready, or willing, to make.

Not only that…it could be dangerous.

Chapter 3

It was late, a blanket of snow hushing the night world outside, but inside her small room Bella was still buzzing from her experience at the restaurant as she opened her Skype contact list, clicked on Hurley's icon, hit Video Call.

Hurley answered on the second ring, his affable features looming live onto her screen, his reddish-brown dreads framing his freckled face, the fishbowl effect of the web-cam making him look even rounder than usual.

"Bella," he said. "Where've you been? I've been trying to get a hold of you for the past forty-eight hours. I have—"

"It's him, Hurley," she said quietly. "The man living in the abbey is Prince Tariq Al Arif. The palace lied about his death. MagMo failed to assassinate him." She spoke in a whisper, a sense of urgency, secrecy taking hold of her.

"Are you certain? Are you ready to run something on the site?"

"I need proof before I break anything. If I send you some

of the high-resolution images of his face, you think you and Scoob could try for a biometrics match?"

"Without a doubt. Scoob's facial-recognition software is top-of-the-line security stuff, Bella. If it's him, we'll get a match. But—"

"Hang on." Bella quickly began loading the digital images into a file. She hit Send, then glanced up registering for the first time a strange sheen of perspiration on Hurley's face.

"Hurley? Is everything okay?"

"Your Watchdog page got another anonymous IM, Bella. Same sender."

"What did it say?"

He rubbed his brow, inhaling deeply. "It was a digital image from an old newspaper. I'm sending it to you now."

Bella clicked on the icon, accepting the file. It opened onto her laptop—an image of two men in black-tie attire, champagne glasses in hand. One of the men was Sam Etherington, taken when he was a lot younger. He had his arm around the shoulders of a dark-haired, stocky guy with receding hairline and a small goatee."

"Who's the guy with Etherington?" Bella said, peering closer.

"Benjamin Raber. The photo ran on the social page of a Chicago newspaper fifteen years ago."

She glanced up, met Hurley's eyes. "Raber? As in Johnson's boss? The head of Strategic Alliances, the alleged front for STRIKE?"

"Same guy."

"Did the tipster say anything about this photo?"

He swallowed, and worry wormed deeper into Bella.

"Hurley, what's going on?"

"All the message said was 'Blackmail is a powerful tool and Johnson was an instrument.'"

"What does that mean?" Bella asked, looking more closely at the two men in the photo, arm in arm. Friends. Celebrating. "That Etherington was blackmailing Raber? Forcing him to use STRIKE—and Johnson—to carry out assassinations?"

"Maybe it's vice versa—Raber blackmailing Etherington."

"Holy Christ," she whispered. "Hurley, we have *got* to find whoever sent these tips. We need more information, we need *proof.* We—"

"Scoob already found her, Bella."

"Her?" Bella whispered.

"She's dead."

Bella's world spun. "What do you mean...dead?"

"This IM with the photo attached appeared on your Watchdog profile just over forty-eight hours ago. Scoob's software trap caught it instantly, and his program started tracking back to her IP address even as she tried to burrow out ahead of the trap. But we got an ID." He swallowed. "Her name was Althea Winston. She was Travis Johnson's widow."

Bella put her hand over her mouth.

"Althea was a computer expert, Bella. Her husband could have told her things no one else would have known. Her tipping us off could have been about revenge for her husband's death, her way of seeking justice for him. But she must've been scared they'd come after her. And now, forty-eight hours after she sent that last IM, she's dead."

Bella's heart began to thud against her rib cage. "How did she die?"

"It was all over the news this morning. Althea and her five-year-old daughter were killed in a freak car accident on the way to the kid's school. Road was icy. They were sideswiped by a gray Dodge Ram 4500, no plates. Impact forced them through the bridge barrier and they went over, through ice, into the river. The truck fled the scene."

Just like the "accident" that had sent Senator Sam Etherington's ex-wife and twins over a bridge.

Looking ill, Hurley said, "Scoob figures someone started monitoring Althea's electronic movements after you posted that photo linking Tariq Al Arif to Alexis Etherington. It must have sent up red flags, and they had to have fingered Johnson's widow as a possible leak. Then when she contacted your page again with this, they had her red-handed."

Bella sat back, horrified. She'd found an old newspaper photograph of the senator's missing ex-wife, Dr. Alexis Etherington, with Dr. Tariq Al Arif at a medical convention in Chicago years ago. She'd posted it online with a story she'd written after Tariq's family had announced his "death." In the caption, she'd suggested there might be old links between the Etheringtons and the Al Arifs. Bella had hoped this hoped this might solicit information, and it had. Now this.

"Jesus, Hurley," Bella whispered. "We killed her. My investigation. This is *my* fault."

"Bella, even if her death is linked to this, it's *not* your fault—Althea had to have known she was taking a risk by tipping you off in the first place. She had to have known they meant serious business after her husband was killed."

"Who the hell is *they,* Hurley! STRIKE? Strategic Alliances? Raber? Sam Etherington's people? Why on earth would Etherington want to kill an Al Arif prince, anyway? He's the one promising an oil deal with their kingdom should he get into office. And how does MagMo fit in to all this?"

"We need to figure all that out before they find *you*." Hurley's features were tight. "This is why I've been try-

ing to get a hold of you—since Scoob's trap chased back
to Althea Winston's IP addy, someone's been trying to use
the same digital trail as a route back into our systems."

Nausea washed through Bella's stomach. "Did they get
in?"

"Not yet. We've increased security parameters. But
they're circling like sharks, and they're going to keep trying to find a way to penetrate our system." Hurley paused,
wiping the gleam from the top of his lip. "It's best you contact us only when really necessary, Bella. You've still got
that prepaid cell?"

"Yes."

"I'm going to get one, too. And I'm using a laptop that's
not connected to our servers to be safe. We'll run these
photos you've just sent through the biometrics software,
then I'm going to shred them, so keep copies on your end.
I'm not going to store anything this side, in case these
people get in."

The gravity of Hurley's words, the news of Althea Winston's death, settled like ice in Bella's chest. Finding that
tipster had been Bella's hope of finding proof, someone
who might eventually go on record. Now she was dead.
Like her husband. Silenced.

"We're up against a wall now, Hurley," she said quietly. "We have nothing concrete to link Etherington to the
attempts on the lives of the Al Arifs. Or to these recent
deaths. Or my attack."

"You still have the fact that Tariq is alive, if these photos
are a match. That's a big story in itself. We run that, and
we could get more tips. Plus Scoob is still trying to clean
up that audio we recorded of Senator Etherington and his
aide, Isaiah Gold, near the fountain last summer. That new
parabolic mike design picked up everything, the trouble is
filtering out the noise of the water."

"The odds of something coming from that audio are practically nonexistent, even if Scoob does manage to clean it up. They could've been discussing baseball for all we know."

"There's a reason Sam and Isaiah routinely leave the office and cross the lawn to talk by a noisy fountain. We think it's to discuss things they don't want on tape. We took photos of them doing it—if we find something on that audio—"

"It's a long shot, Hurley. You guys have made a hobby of eavesdropping on politicians with your gimmicks for years, and what have you got so far?"

His mouth flattened, and she instantly felt sorry.

"I'm sorry. It's just…I'm rattled about Althea's death."

"We all are. Go get the sheik, Bella. Get him to talk. Somehow this all ties back to Sam."

She signed off, shut her laptop and sat staring into space awhile. Outside the snow continued to fall. She'd survived her attack. Althea Winston had not been so lucky. Had it been the same people?

Bella's assailants had spoken Arabic and she figured they might be part of MagMo. Two of them also had Arabic daggers. But this wouldn't fit Sam Etherington's people.

Bella reached into her pocket and took out a small, gold medallion. She'd ripped it from the neck of one of her assailants as she'd tried to fight him off.

The medallion depicted a sun superimposed by a hooked dagger, and it lay warm in her hand, the gold gleaming dully in the light from her lamp. She hadn't shown it to the police—the cops had been no help when her apartment had been ransacked, and by that point, Bella trusted no one.

It was also when she'd fled the country.

Slipping the medallion onto a chain around her neck, she turned up the oil heater and climbed under the duvet on her small cot. She lay there, feeling alone, vulnerable. Scared. This story was potentially so big it overwhelmed her.

She muttered a curse. She was a journalist. This was everything she'd wanted, surely—an earth-shattering scoop? And when something truly scared you, it generally meant you were heading in the right direction. Wasn't that the mantra of self-help gurus?

This was going to be her ticket back into the mainstream, her revenge against the *Daily* for dumping her. She wanted to shove this story in Derek's face, show him she was worth something. She wanted the whole world to see Bella DiCaprio was not some little orphan cast-off. She was someone to be reckoned with.

A familiar, stubborn anger filled Bella, and determination steeled her. She was not averse to risk. She was going to get this. The trick would be in finding a way to get the sheik to talk to her, to find out how much he knew, and how this might all be connected.

And tomorrow was her chance, when she went to see him in the abbey.

The following afternoon found Bella pushing her bike through several inches of snow for the last mile to the monastery. The wind off the Atlantic was biting, the sky low and somber. Hurley's words threaded through her mind.

We need to figure out who they are before they find you...

She rounded a hill of rock and the stone walls of the abbey suddenly loomed in the distance, black and menacing under skiffs of white. It would be full dark within the hour, she thought. A bite of raw fear twisted into her sense of foreboding.

What if her assailants back in D.C. *were* linked to Tariq's people—would his family kill to keep his secret?

Would they come after her if they knew she was here, on the island, now?

As she reached the iron gates, her fingers felt numb on the handlebars despite the gloves she wore. And another, more sinister thought niggled into her mind—what if Tariq's reason for suddenly summoning her to his monastery was to silence her?

Her attackers in D.C. *had* spoken Arabic. And they had carried traditional-looking curved daggers. Sam's people would not have done so, surely?

She paused and looked up at the row of hostile iron spikes, thinking of the gold medallion in her pocket—the image of a sun, superimposed with a hooked Arabic dagger. The wind was picking up and it had started snowing again, tiny ice crystals pricking into her face. Bella reached up and pressed the intercom in the stone pillar on the right side of the gate. A bell clanged somewhere inside the monastery, resonant, distant, an ancient sound that seemed at odds with the modern security. Her gaze was pulled up to the high-tech motion-sensor cameras watching her. Anxiety wrapped around Bella.

She told herself to relax. It was unlikely Tariq knew who she was at this point. But her alias *was* superficial—it wouldn't hold up to any real background investigation. She needed to get to the heart of the reason she was here sooner rather than later.

Bella waited almost a full minute. Snow came down faster now, angled by the wind.

She rang again, and at the sound of the clanging something moved under the blanket in her bike basket. With a sharp start Bella realized she'd almost forgotten the Papillon pup Madame had insisted she take with her if she wanted time off this evening.

"Kiki needs attention and exercise, Amelie," Madame

Dubois had said. "This is why I hired you. If you want to go to the abbey, you will need to take Kiki."

The Papillon was not the only thing Bella had been obliged to trek up the hill this evening—in the carrier on the back of her bike was a hamper, which Madame had shoved into her hands as she left.

"What's this?" Bella had asked.

"The way to a man's heart, Amelie—" Madame said, nodding to the hamper "—is always through his stomach. Take the basket."

"I'm not looking for a way into anyone's heart," Bella had responded irritably. At the same time she reminded herself to play along. If Estelle Dubois believed in her eccentric old mind that Bella was romantically interested in the mysterious stranger from the abbey, it could make coming up here a lot easier.

Bella lifted the edge of the blanket. Kiki poked her nose out into the cold, giving a little body wiggle and whimper. "Hang on," she whispered to the pup. "You can run around when we get inside."

As she spoke the iron gates suddenly began to creak open, no one in sight. A frisson of nerves chased over her skin.

She began to wheel her bike through the gates and up to the great stone entrance, her tires making narrow tracks behind her in the slush.

Stone columns flanked a double door of heavy wood that was carved with warring demons and angels and arched to a point. The handles were iron rings.

As Bella approached, the door opened a crack and a slice of pale yellow light spliced the gloom. A butler with dark complexion and hooded eyes appeared, unsmiling.

"I'm Amelie Chenard," she said, unnerved by the inhospitable set of the man's features. "Monsieur Du Val is expecting me."

He gave a barely perceptible tip of his head and stepped back, making room for her to enter. Bella rested her bike against the wall and removed Kiki from the basket. She asked the butler to bring in the hamper from the back of the bike.

With a deadpan expression, he removed the basket and Bella followed him into a massive hall. The ceilings were vaulted, high. A massive iron chandelier hung from a chain above a thick wood table in the center of the hall. Fat candles burned in sconces along the walls. The air inside was cold and had a strange weight to it. Clearly, central heating had not been part of the refurbishment.

"Monsieur is waiting in the library," the butler said, setting her hamper on the table. "If I can take your coat?" He held out a dark-skinned hand.

"Could you hold this for me?" She offered Kiki to him.

The butler's eyes flashed up, meeting hers properly for the first time.

"The dog?"

"Please, so I can take off my coat."

Uneasy, the man took the ball of wriggling fur, holding Kiki at arm's length as she tried to lick his face. Bella shrugged out of her slicker and removed her hat, holding them out to the butler. He called out for assistance.

Another male servant came hurrying into the hallway, looking surprised as the butler handed him the dog and muttered in French for him to watch it while Mademoiselle Chenard visited with the Monsieur. Bella took note of their accents as they conversed. Both rolled their *r*'s low in their throats in the way of Arabic.

"Her name is Kiki," she called out after the man as he turned to leave with the dog. He shot a dark glance over his shoulder. Bella smiled inwardly and said a silent thank-you to Madame Dubois as she followed the butler down a wide and dimly lit stone corridor. The dog was easing her tension.

The air in this part of the abbey smelled slightly musty, like an old church. The butler stopped to open a thick wooden door, showing Bella into a library.

She entered cautiously. The room was massive but warm, with lots of rich wood paneling. Bookshelves lined the walls, floor to ceiling. A cello stood at one end of the room, the smooth wood gleaming from the light of a fire that crackled softly in a big stone hearth. Persian rugs in rich reds and rust browns covered the floors. At the far end of the room another door opened into what looked like a study—Bella could see a desk of polished black wood. On it rested a stubby phone—satellite phone, she guessed—along with a pile of papers.

"Mademoiselle Chenard," the butler announced before sliding quietly away and closing the door.

Tariq stood up from the chair he'd been seated in next to the fire. The size of the wingback had hidden him from view. He turned slowly to face her.

Bella's heart stilled as last summer's headlines flooded through her mind.

Heir to Al Na'Jar Throne Dead. Renowned Surgeon Prince Dies. Prince Assassinated. Palace Mourns...

And here he was.

Already she could see the new headlines.

Sheik Al Arif Found Alive. Palace Lied. MagMo failed to Assassinate Heir. Al Na'Jar Prince Found Recovering in France.

She could also imagine the photographs she'd taken of him on the cliff splashed over news pages, and a disturbing little thought entered her mind. Why break this story on the Watchdog site—why not take it straight to one of the major media outlets? It would be her byline, her photo credits. Then she thought of Hurley, Scoob, Agnes, all the investigative legwork they'd done to help her get to this point. Guilt wormed into her.

"Come in," he said, his voice rich, resonant. Deep.

Bella swallowed and took a few steps forward, tension tightening in her stomach.

He stepped around the chair, facing her square. He wore black pants—expensively cut, perfectly pressed. His white shirt was open at the neck showing a silk cravat. His hair was a glossy raven in the firelight. The eye patch lent him an air of mystery. In spite of his scars his presence shimmered with intensity, authority, wealth and something charismatically—and darkly—seductive.

Bella's gaze settled on his mouth, the way his lip turned down on the left. An earlier photograph of him shifted to mind—Tariq smiling as he accepted a polo trophy, his teeth stark white against dusky skin. The photographer had captured a fire that had burned bright in his black eyes that day. Bella wondered if he *could* still smile, or if that ability, too, had been stolen from him by MagMo terrorists.

She came a little closer, holding out her hand. "I'm Amelie—"

"Amelie Chenard," he said, lifting his chin slightly and clasping his own hands behind his back. He made no move toward her. She dropped her hand back to her side, feeling awkward, and wondered if he was hiding his maimed hand this way. What did it take for a man once so devastatingly good-looking, so talented a neurosurgeon, to deal with this change in his body, his life?

"You work for Estelle Dubois," he said. "You're here to do research for a novel." He paused, watching her intently. "Or so I am told."

"Yes," she said simply, waiting to see where he was going to take this.

"This would be your debut novel." It wasn't a question.

She smiled, warmly. Or so she hoped. "So, you've looked me up?"

He said nothing.

Apprehension rose in her.

Before she'd left the States, Hurley and Scoob had managed to create a basic internet presence for "Amelie Chenard," but it was superficial. Anyone digging deeper would soon see that. Bella had been lucky to secure her job with Estelle Dubois only two days after her arrival on Ile-en-Mer, and she'd managed to do it without applying for permits of any sort. She also hadn't used her passport or any ID since arriving in France via the Chunnel, and so far she hadn't touched the credit cards hidden in her room alongside her passport and driver's license.

"Yes, it will be my first, at least under my own name, should it be published." She tried to hold her smile. "If you did look up my website you'll have seen that I've worked as a ghost writer to date, but contracts have bound me to confidentiality as to whom I've written for."

His gaze bored into her, hot, intense. She tried not to blink, to look away. But her skin heated.

Still, he remained silent, waiting.

She cleared her throat. "I grew tired of being in the shadows all the time," she said. "I want to step out, do something for myself, make my own name. Hence the new website, and now, my own book." Bella hoped this would explain the apparent lack of internet litter around her alias. "It's why I came to France, to this island. For the research. And I thought it might be good to stay awhile, absorb the local culture, the rhythms of the people."

His butler appeared like a ghost, startling Bella—she

hadn't even heard the door open. He set Madame's hamper on a table near the fire, then left. The sheik didn't even glance at his servant, or the hamper.

Silently Bella thanked Madame again—clearly she was going to need a diversion, something to break the fortress of ice this man had built around himself. She glanced at the hamper, wondering what was inside.

"Your French is good," he said abruptly.

"Thank you. I minored in French and philosophy."

"Where?"

Perspiration suddenly prickled over her body. "Seattle," she lied. It was the first place that came to mind that was not Chicago or D.C., and she'd visited the university there so she knew something about it.

"What was your major?"

"Literature," she lied again, then forced a light laugh. "You're making me feel as though I pushed my bike all the way up here simply to be interrogated."

His features remained implacable. "You've been following me, Amelie. I want to know why."

"I think it's pretty obvious," she said quietly, her smile dying on her lips. "I was hoping for a tour of the abbey, and I wanted to ask you about the ghost, the history of the place." Silence hung between them. The fire crackled and popped, giving a slight hiss.

"Is Seattle your home, Amelie?"

She swallowed the panic ballooning in her throat. "Yes."

"You were born there?"

"Portland, Oregon." She cursed herself even as the words came out of her mouth. She was just digging a deeper hole for herself. She had to open up real channels of communication before he dug further into her background and discovered she was a fake.

"And you decided to come live in France while you researched this idea for a novel?"

"You manage to make that sound condescending."

"I'm sorry."

He didn't sound it.

"It was more than just the research," she said, cutting closer to the truth now. "I had some personal issues, a recent breakup with a man I thought I loved, and I needed to get away for a while."

Damn, why was she even going there? She spoke too much when she was nervous.

Something crossed his features, then was gone—she'd gotten through to him, briefly.

"I don't appreciate being followed, Amelie," he said finally, more gently.

"I really did try a more conventional approach—I rang the bell at the gate twice, but there was no answer. I asked around the village if anyone had a phone number for the abbey. Then Madame Dubois said you liked to walk along the cliffs in the afternoon, so I followed you on the heath." She paused. "I confess, after seeing you standing at the edge of the cliffs, I became curious beyond the book research. I wanted to meet you."

"To see firsthand the beast who lives in a haunted stone monastery on the cliffs—to see his scars? Is that why you took photographs of me, inspiration for your *gothic* novel?"

The bitterness—the rawness in his voice—was a shock, a punch to her gut. "That's not—"

"Not what the villagers think of me—the scarred monster in the haunted abbey?"

Bella inhaled deeply. "I'm not even going to dignify that with an answer." She pointed her arm in the direction of the village. "Those locals have nothing but respect for you and your privacy. They treat you like a revered guest on this island—"

"Because I have money."

She dropped her hand, stared.

"Think about it, Amelie. The trappings of wealth are all I have left. They buy me a measure of dignity. They allow me privacy."

She heard the subtext—he could no longer work as a surgeon, no longer play his cello, win his polo matches… he'd lost the love of his life, the desire to help run his country. He needed to be alone.

"And so you hide," she said quietly, "behind your wealth, in a remote abbey because you don't want people to see your face, because you think you're somehow damaged?"

He studied her, his presence seeming to glower with a dark, angry, yet magnetic power.

"How did it happen, Tahar?"

Something tore sharp and fast across the one side of his face, a ghost of an emotion, there, then gone, as if she might have imagined it. The other side of his face remained immobile, stiff. It was as if his psyche was split in two—a modern-day Jekyll and Hyde.

Her heart hammered. Perhaps she'd stepped over the line. But Bella told herself it was a normal question from someone who had nothing to hide. And he was the one who'd broached the subject by referring to himself as a "scarred beast of a man."

But his gaze, his energy, was so intense, crackling, dark, she felt her cheeks go hot and she looked away. "I'm sorry. That was forward. I don't need to know. I only wanted to—"

"It was a car accident," he said abruptly. "I was in a coma for a while afterward."

Surprise rippled through her. She opened her mouth

but words eluded her. In her mind she could see Derek's photo, Tariq fleeing the burning jet, such fierceness, such pain in his eyes as he tried to save his fiancée. Guilt sliced through her and she cursed the hungry newshound inside her own body.

"I'm so sorry," she said. "I…there are no easy words for something like this. And I suspect you don't want platitudes, anyway."

"You're right, I don't." He strode over to the hamper on the table, opened the lid of the wicker hamper as he spoke. "What did you bring?"

"Actually it's from Madame Dubois. I have no idea what's in there."

He pulled out a bottle of Chateau Luneau cabernet franc and his gaze ticked to hers. "She knows what I like," he said very quietly. "And so do you—this is what you were drinking in the restaurant."

Tension shimmered. A piece of wet wood hissed in the fire, and Bella could hear wind moaning up in the turrets somewhere. She thought she could also hear the distant crash of waves at the foot of the cliffs upon which they were perched, the rhythmic thrust of the Atlantic—a pulse as old as time. She shook herself.

"Madame Dubois told me about the wine," she said quietly. "She also told me you dined at Le Grotte every Tuesday night. I went there to meet you. I had hoped to strike up conversation through the wine, and then ask for a tour of the abbey." She forced a laugh, but it felt hollow. "The wine just about broke my budget."

A twitch of amusement ran along the right side of his mouth. Or had she imagined it? Whatever it was, something seemed to shift in the color of the evening.

From the hamper he removed a round of cheese and a box of crackers. He set them on the table. Reaching in again, he pulled out two wineglasses and a corkscrew. He held the glasses up, crooked his brow.

Ridiculously, Bella felt her cheeks flush again. She told herself it was the warmth of the fire finally getting through after her cold ride. Yet there was something so damn sensual about this dark, damaged man, something so barely restrained it overwhelmed her, and more. It set her nerves tingling for the feel of his touch against her skin.

"Madame insisted I bring the hamper," she said, her voice thickening. "Estelle Dubois maintains the way to a man's heart is through his stomach. She seems to think every single woman must be in search of a male." Even as the words came out her mouth she wished she could take them back. Bella was suddenly floundering, in part, she realized, because she'd been attracted to Tariq—both physically and mentally—long before this moment.

To find him alive, to actually be in his powerful presence, was rattling her. Because Tariq Al Arif in the flesh more than exceeded Bella's expectations. Everything about him exuded the aura of a Saharan prince from an exotic country steeped in ancient, desert tradition, and standing so near him, she didn't feel quite real. Again she felt like an Alice that had slipped through some kind of fairy-tale looking glass. Bella in the castle with the scarred "beast" of a prince.

"And you're not?"

She coughed, eyes watering. "Not what?"

"Looking for a man."

The heat in her cheeks deepened and she felt irritated by her body's betrayal. "Like I said, I had a bad breakup with my ex. I came to get away from all that, quite frankly."

"So it was serious, this relationship of yours?"

"I thought it was."

Tariq angled his head slightly, reading her. Then he set

the wineglasses on the table, picked up the bottle of wine and the corkscrew.

Turning his back to her he struggled to uncork the bottle.

Bella went quickly up to him. "Here, let me." She reached out, taking the bottle and opener from him. Her hand brushed against his skin as she did, and heat shocked through her. Bella froze, met his eye.

Anger crackled from him in waves. She understood. He'd been a top neurosurgeon and now he couldn't even open a bottle of wine without fumbling.

"I can see you're left-handed," she said softly, averting her eyes from his crippled fingers, focusing instead on twisting the corkscrew, heat still rippling through her. "It must be difficult—" she popped the cork "—adjusting to the use of a nondominant hand."

A muscle began to work at his jaw.

She poured the wine, handed him a glass, careful not to connect with his skin again.

"Will you ever fully regain use of your left hand?" she said quietly.

Will you ever operate again, play the cello, ride a horse...

He stared at her, intense, silent. Bella began to feel self-conscious.

"I apologize—I'm stepping out of my bounds tonight. What I really—"

"I might regain all the refinement of a wooden club," he said, taking a deep swallow of his wine. She watched his Adam's apple move under dusky skin. "If I do the physiotherapy."

Madame's words sifted into Bella's mind.

A private ferry came over from the mainland with gymnasium equipment. A woman came with it... I think she had

something to do with the gymnasium equipment, perhaps a
personal trainer. But she left very abruptly, the next day...

He'd fired his physiotherapist.

"You're not doing the exercises?"

He turned and strode to the fire, stared into the flames,
glass in hand, firelight dancing in the burgundy liquid.

"To put it simply," he said, still facing the fire, his voice
low and deep in his throat. "The brain-to-limb connection
is one of the hardest to regain. Sometimes, I'll be holding
an object in my left hand, then I get distracted, and the
thing just drops from my fingers because the neurologi-
cal connection is missing."

"So you're not even trying," she said softly.

He spun round abruptly, his features hard.

"I came to this island for one thing, Amelie. Privacy.
I'll tell you what you want, then leave me alone. Please."

She inhaled deeply, a tightening in her stomach.

Don't blow it, Bella....

"Okay," she said quietly. "I'd like to ask you about the
ghost of the abbess. Have you—"

"There is no ghost. It's a legend born out of a tragic
historical event."

She nodded, moistening her lips, thinking of Ambassador Pierre Belard and how he'd told her that Julie, as a
child, had been fascinated with the abbey ghost stories.

"I was wondering if perhaps any of your staff might
have seen or heard the—"

"The winter wind blows down the Atlantic from the
northwest," he said curtly. "When it reaches a certain velocity, it moans through the old turrets and spires. At a
greater velocity the sound pitches to a blood-curdling
scream. That's all there is to it."

"Well, I find the history of the abbey and the murder of—"

"You don't need me to research the history of the invasions of Brittany, Amelie, or the death of the abbess. It's well documented. There's also a small museum on the outskirts of the village. You can get what you need from the curator there."

Bella set her glass down.

"Fair enough," she said quietly, sensing her time here was running out, and fast. "Were her bones really buried in the dungeons? Are they still there?"

"The dungeons have not been refurbished. If the abbess was indeed entombed down there, she's still there."

The wind moaned louder suddenly and a chill rippled over Bella's skin. Was it her imagination, or had the temperature inside just dropped?

"Must be strange," she prompted, "living on top of the history of a violent death. Some people think stone holds memory, that if you touch it you can feel things from the past. Do you ever feel…anything?"

Tariq snorted. If only she knew how deeply he felt everything, how hard he was trying to stay numb. She had no idea what violence he and his family and his country lived with on a daily basis—what the bomb blast had ripped from him.

"If there is pain and violence in these walls, if there is a ghost in this abbey, I don't feel it." He snorted softly. "But that might be because the abbess has no reason to haunt *me*."

He was already haunted. Cold, dead to the outside world. Except he wasn't cold right now—he'd felt the electricity in Amelie's touch when her hand brushed his, the heat that had speared to his groin. The way his pulse had quickened at the sight of her short skirt that showed far too much long leg for his comfort. He was not immune to the subtle scent of her perfume, or the fragrance of the shampoo in her hair. The way her bright fuchsia sweater hugged her rounded breasts. The way her dark curls framed her heart-shaped face and looked soft to the touch.

Amelie reminded him of sex. Of when he last had it, how much he enjoyed it. How desperately his body craved hers right now—naked and warm and wrapped around him.

He didn't want to think about sex. Especially with Amelie.

He wanted to remember, to honor, Julie. His hand fisted around his glass.

"You're right," she was saying. "I can do the historical research elsewhere, and I have. I was just hoping for more."

Silence swelled between them. The moan of the wind outside rose and fell and the fire crackled.

She bit her bottom lip, nodded. "I see." She turned to leave, then spun back suddenly. "Why *did* you even invite me here? Just to interrogate me?"

"Yes," he said quietly.

"And did you get what you want?"

In spite of himself he felt a stab of guilt.

"Yes." He'd gotten information about where she claimed to have been born, lived, attended university, what she'd studied. It was enough to start a decent background check. He'd get Omair going on that immediately, because he didn't trust her.

Or was it that he didn't trust himself, his own body, how much he desired her? Was he hoping Omair would find something nefarious, so that he could redirect his lust into anger?

Because if there were something to find, Omair would find it. His brother had access to the best contract intelligence in the business, as well as a top private investigator in the States.

In the meantime—while Omair's people were digging—it perhaps *would* be better to keep her close, keep the lines of communication open, until he could be certain. Because if she was somehow connected to his enemies, they might be able to use her to find The Moor.

Reluctance, conflict, swirled through him. Close proximity was one thing, but how long before his control cracked?

Tariq inhaled and bit the bullet.

"My men will give you a tour of the abbey tomorrow morning. Be here at ten. They will answer any questions they can. You may take photographs, and then I expect to be left alone."

This was a good compromise—he wouldn't necessarily have to see her again himself, but he'd have opportunity if he needed it.

Her violet eyes widened, lambent in the firelight. "Thank you, Tahar," she said softly.

He inclined his head slightly.

The wind in the turrets outside rose to a high-pitched scream that came down the chimney. He saw the way she glanced up, knew she was thinking of the abbess. She rubbed her hand over her arm. "The snow must really be coming down now."

He nodded. "Yes. It's best you leave while a vehicle can still get through. My men will take you."

She met his eyes. "Can I ask you one more question before I go?"

He angled his head.

"Why did you buy this place?"

He was silent for a long time, memories suddenly cutting through him. The abbey had been Julie's engagement present. She'd been fascinated with the place as a child, and it had filled Tariq's heart with happiness to be able to gift it to her. They'd planned to spend summers here, during the opera festival.

Images of children, sunshine, salt breezes filled his mind—their dreams. Dashed. The scream of the wind grew to a wail, washing the images away. Waves boomed and somewhere windows rattled as if vengeful spirits were seeking a way in.

"I bought it for someone I loved."

She swallowed, a strange look in her eyes.

He inhaled deeply, tension straining his shoulders. "She's no longer with me."

"The accident?"

"Yes. Her death was my fault." He was unable to stop the words that welled out from deep inside. "I'm a doctor, Amelie. And I could not save her."

She paled. "That…that doesn't make it your fault, Tahar." She was speaking from a raw place now, filled with compassion, and he felt a sudden bond, something real.

"It was my fault for loving her," he said. "If she hadn't been with me—"

"Please." She reached out, touched his crippled hand. Sympathy gleamed in her eyes and her skin was cool against his. "Don't do this to yourself, Tahar. You can't blame yourself for something like this."

He gave a slight shrug and moved out from under her touch. He didn't want Amelie's sympathy, didn't want to feel a bond. "Now I live in her abbey. So you see, the abbess doesn't need to bother with me. I'm haunted by my own memories. I don't need her ghost to remind me of the purgatory in which I hang."

She stared at him. The wind screamed louder. Tariq held himself dead still, focusing on controlling his emotions, on holding the wineglass in his crippled hand. But the strain of it all was making him shake inside.

He shouldn't have said these things.

And now, telling Amelie the veiled truth had given rise to a fierce and terrible need to lean on someone, to share his grief, to feel a human connection again, even as he fought against it. Because of this he wanted suddenly to lash out at her for making things raw again.

"You should go."

But before Amelie could move, the library door edged open and in came a little yellow-and-white dog with huge, tufted, batlike ears. It bounded over Tariq's Persian carpet in a rocking-horse motion as it made straight for Amelie. Surprise rippled through Tariq.

"Kiki!" She crouched down and held out her arms. "What are you doing in here, you little monster?" The animal leaped into her arms, and she ruffled its fur. Tariq couldn't help noticing how the firelight lent burgundy highlights to Amelie's hair. How finely boned her pale-skinned hands were. How her skirt rode up her lean, stockinged thighs as she crouched down. He felt his body harden.

And he was suddenly desperate for her to leave. She'd outstayed her welcome—it was about all he could take.

"I'm sorry," she said, glancing up at him with those purple eyes. "Madame insisted I bring Kiki if I wanted time off. I think she hired me mostly for the dogs." She gave him a big grin, and so help him, seeing that cute little gap between her front teeth awakened something ferocious and carnal in him. Something he might not be able to shut down now that it had been released. His groin began to pulse with a heat and life he'd all but forgotten.

"I asked your butler to take care of her but I guess she got away." As she spoke the little ball of fur wriggled free from Amelie's hands, bounded toward Tariq and jumped up against his pant legs. Tariq stared down at the dog, refusing to touch it. Refusing to move at all.

But it kept on hopping, and then it started yipping.

Finally he set his wineglass on the mantel, then crouched down and stroked the animal. The fur under his palm was soft as silk. Excited by the attention the pup leaped to his face and licked him.

Tariq smiled, in spite of himself.

Amelie laughed in response—a warm, husky sound that curled right through his stomach. He froze, stared at her. They were now both crouched on the floor. He could see the dark delta of space between her stockinged thighs. And he could see her registering his noticing this.

Her smile faded as she met his gaze, her purple eyes darkening. And the awareness of some undercurrent of mutual sexual attraction shimmered hot and thick into the silence between them. And suddenly Tariq hurt—every nerve in his body in pain, as if thawing out from a deep frost as lust burned up from his belly, seared through his chest, tingled into his fingertips, tightened his throat.

The intensity, the raw, primal, physical yearning for this young, vital woman in front of him was overwhelming, clouding his logic. And the intensity of it scared him. He lurched to his feet, reaching for anger, rage, anything that would shut out this feeling, help him leash and control it.

"You need to leave, at once," he said curtly. "I have another appointment."

She stood, very slowly, a look of understanding sifting into those big eyes. She knew. She could see what she was doing to him.

That made it worse.

It gave her power over him. Tariq preferred the power, the control, to be entirely in his hands.

He called out for his butler. The man appeared instantly at the door.

"Get the driver to take Mademoiselle Chenard home."

"And the bicycle, Monsieur?"

"She can fetch it when she returns tomorrow."

Amelie picked up Kiki, holding the dog close against her breasts. "Thank you, Tahar." She hesitated, something unreadable entering her eyes as she glanced at his cello at the far end of the room. "You should work on that hand, you know. I'd love to hear you play your cello one day."

The anger inside him erupted. He was a neurosurgeon. He knew his limitations. He didn't need this young woman to tell him what to do. Turning his back on her he went to stand in front of the fire, his entire body vibrating.

He heard the door close behind him.

And the library felt suddenly hollow, as if she'd sucked all the warmth out with her.

Tariq reached for his glass of wine, downed the remainder in one, angry go.

He'd made a mistake inviting her here.

He'd wanted to take control of this situation, of her, then send her away. Instead he'd managed to invite her in deeper, allowing her to crack through the ice of his emotional defenses, his grief. And Tariq had a sinking feeling he had no way of controlling what was seeping out from those cracks now.

Chapter 4

Aban Ghaffar, renowned billionaire industrialist, a man who owned half of Manhattan and had steered countless political campaigns, studied the enlarged digital image on his computer screen, a silent fury burning into his gut.

"Where did you get this?" he said, very quietly, into his phone.

"My surveillance team accessed the Watchdog servers via a backdoor virus, using the same digital trail they used to track Althea Winston's messages. The team doesn't know we're in there, watching every keystroke. This photo and others like it were uploaded and run through a sophisticated facial-recognition software program." Isaiah Gold's voice was measured, devoid of emotion, as it usually was.

"He was supposed to be killed in the bombing."

"She found him. Alive."

"Where?"

"We don't know yet."

Aban, alias The Moor, stared out at the city skyline. Skyscraper lights like jewels against velvet stretched out below his penthouse windows.

Usually the sight calmed him, but not tonight. Sam Etherington's special aide, Isaiah Gold, was working under the radar with him on this project to overthrow Al Na'Jar, keeping the senator on a need-to-know basis for his political protection. Gold had also provided Aban with some men who'd partnered with his MagMo operatives in D.C. But they'd failed to abduct—or kill—journalist Bella Di-Caprio, and they'd been hunting for her ever since she appeared to have fled the States.

All they knew was that she'd boarded a plane, landed at Heathrow in the U.K., then vanished. Now she'd found Sheik Tariq Al Arif. Alive.

The Moor's attempts to assassinate the next in line of succession to the Al Na'Jar throne had clearly failed. Aban did not tolerate failure. His only concession was that they'd so far managed to eliminate the younger brother, Omair.

"Northern hemisphere," he said quietly into the phone as he scrutinized the image of the scarred man on his screen. "This photo was taken in cold weather. A place with thick fog along a coast. I'll look into this."

"And we'll keep monitoring the Watchdog phone lines and the computers linked to their server," Gold said. "They'll slip. They'll lead us to DiCaprio, and to Tariq Al Arif, eventually."

"Eventually" was not soon enough.

The Moor glanced over his shoulder at his son, Amal, idly flicking through a magazine on a glass coffee table in the penthouse living room.

"If you get a location," he said, watching Amal, "I want to know immediately."

"And vice versa," said Gold.

He hung up.

"Amal!"

His son glanced up, eyes as black as his mother's. He had his mother's brains as well, unfortunately. Aban would have preferred more of his own intellect and drive in the boy. He needed a worthy heir to the colossal underground empire he himself had built from the ground up.

"Pack your bags," he told his son, curtly. "You leave for Paris tonight, on the private jet. Take three men of your choosing with you."

Amal raised a brow. "What's happening?"

"Tariq Al Arif is alive."

Amal's body straightened. *"Alive?"*

"And in hiding. I believe somewhere Europe. Somewhere with access to the ocean. Possibly France—the Al Arif Corporation is based out of Paris and the family has holdings in that country."

The Moor returned his attention to his computer. "This photo of Tariq," he said quietly, "was shot at 4:50 p.m. on Monday. When you get to Paris, I want you to get hold of meteorological data from that day and time, including satellite weather images. I want to know what parts of coastal Europe were clear, what parts had fog at precisely this time."

"That's a huge—"

"It's a start," he said coolly. "A process of elimination. When we find him, I want you close, ready to move on a second's notice."

Amal stared at him. "You want *me* to assassinate—"

"You're my only son—this is your legacy. This is your chance to take a leadership role." He met the boy's gaze. "Don't let me down."

* * *

That night Tariq went into his pool room. He didn't bother switching on the lights. It was warm inside—humid, even. Omair had instructed the abbey staff to keep the water heated even though Tariq had refused to use the pool. Omair was hoping he'd come round, though, and wanted no obstacles in his brother's path to healing.

Tariq walked the length of the lap pool toward the floor-to-ceiling windows that looked out over the cliff. The water shimmered like black oil, reflecting the pearly-black coating beneath the surface. He stopped at the windows, where the water flowed under the glass to the outside section of the pool. An infinity edge gave the illusion of black water vanishing over the cliff.

Wind ruffled the outside surface and steam rose into the snowy night. Tariq inhaled deeply—he'd spent a small fortune in the structural engineering of this pool, and it had been mostly for Julie who swam to keep her sleek shape. In the summer the glass could be moved aside for indoor-outdoor access, and it was the summers that he and Julie had intended to spend here.

Crouching down, he tested the temperature with his hand. The water felt rounded, like silk. Warm.

Putting only the muted underwater lights on, Tariq removed his clothes and slowly slipped naked into the water. It closed softly around him like a familiar lover. He started to swim, awkward at first. But gradually, as his muscles began to loosen, and his body warmed, his heart beat faster and he began to glide through the water, buoyancy helping him find a balance between his crippled half and his good half. He swam hard, harder, working on unison, until his entire body ached with the exertion, and his lungs burned. And it felt good.

It was the first time he'd used the pool.

It was also the first time that the broken part of himself felt so much more aligned with the healthy side, both mentally and physically. And he felt stronger for it.

He pulled himself out and tied a towel around his waist, glancing briefly at the unused gym equipment behind glass on the other side of the room. Tariq held out his clawed hand, tried to flex and close his fingers. With surprise he realized he actually had a little more mobility after the exercise.

You should work on that hand, you know. I'd love to hear you play your cello one day...

The depression began to sink into him again—an insidious blackness.

Tariq showered and dressed, then went into his office off the library. His butler had stoked the fire and it crackled in the hearth.

Seating himself at his computer, he looked up Amelie Chenard's website and reread her bio.

It all seemed to fit with what she'd told him.

Clicking through her social media profiles he studied the photographs of her. She wasn't beautiful, not by any traditional stretch, but alluring, and sexually compelling. The was something irreverent about her looks, a quirky dress sense evident in these photos. At times there was a playfulness in her big purple eyes, at other times they showed a pensive intelligence. And as he studied the images, the now-familiar surge of anger and attraction braided around his heart. He leaned back in his chair, her words sifting back into his mind.

I'd love to hear you play the cello one day...

He hadn't told her he used to play. But the cello standing in his library could have prompted her comment. An uneasiness twisted through Tariq.

He leaned forward and quickly did an internet search, pairing her name with keywords like *Seattle, university.* Nothing came up. He worked backward—Amelie was probably around twenty-eight. A decade ago, when she'd most likely have started university, people didn't have the kind of online presence they did now. And if she'd gone into ghostwriting right after graduating, she could conceivably have had good reason to keep a low internet profile due to contractual obligations to secrecy.

Tariq ran his hand over his damp hair, then reached for his encrypted sat phone and dialed Omair. As he listened to the phone ring, he thought of his brother's partner, Faith, and their tiny newborn he had never seen. Guilt closed like a noose around his neck. He should have called earlier, asked how they were doing.

Omair and Faith were staying temporarily on the Force du Sable base. The private army for which Omair contracted occupied the small island of Sao Diogo off the coast of Angola, along with a handful of locals. Most of the F.D.S. military contractors lived on the island, some of them with families. After taking Faith home to meet the royal family in Al Na'Jar, Omair decided it was safer to move her to Sao Diogo to wait out the rest of her pregnancy and give birth. They still did not know whether it was the U.S. government who'd tried to kill her, or a rogue faction within STRIKE, the dark ops hit squad for which Faith used to work.

Either way, whoever had come after her believed they'd succeeded in killing both Faith and Omair in a yacht explosion off the coast of Western Sahara.

Omair wanted to keep it that way. At least until they figured out who was actually behind the assassination attempts, and who had killed Faith's handler, Travis Johnson, in D.C. Or until The Moor was unveiled and his MagMo followers defeated.

Meanwhile, Faith had given birth to a baby boy almost two weeks ago. It struck Tariq that he didn't even recall the baby's name. Self-recrimination sliced through him. He really should have called earlier, asked how Faith and the child were doing.

There was no answer and his call went to voice mail. Tariq glanced at his watch. In Arabic he left a message asking after Faith and the baby. He did not mention the real reason for his call. When Omair returned his message, Tariq would ask him to investigate Amelie, but only once he'd made sure mother and child were well.

He hung up and stared into space.

Never in his wildest dreams had Tariq thought his mercenary brother, the dark horse in the family, would make a family before he did. As happy as he was for his brother, it drove home the depth of his own loss. His incredible loneliness.

He got up from his desk and went into the library, turning off the lights as he headed for bed.

But he stopped in front of the fire.

Embers glowed red, orange, pulsing in the darkness.

He watched the coals for a while. Then on impulse, he took his cello from its stand and sat by the fire, the instrument positioned between his knees. Like the unused pool that had been kept heated, the unused cello had been kept tuned. Clutching the brazilwood bow awkwardly in his clawed left hand, Tariq stroked it over the strings, the sound sonorous, hollow. He closed his eyes, trying to concentrate on moving the bow the way he once used to, aching to feel the music rise from the cello, reverberate in his chest, fill his heart and mind. But instead the image of the burning jet—the searing heat, the odor of burnt flesh and singed hair—slammed into his mind. And painful memories looped over and over.

He could feel Julie in his arms again, see her lying on the tarmac, her eyes open, unseeing. He could hear screaming. He felt his body, his mind, every molecule in his being trying to revive her. The utter despair in being unable to save her.

His hands stilled and tears leaked from his good eye.

Softly, Tariq swore in Arabic. Amelie had done this. *She'd* made him care again. She'd made him get into the pool, to ache for the taste of harmony in his body again. She'd forced him to call his family and butt up against his own guilt and self-recrimination for not having done so earlier.

She'd made him hold his cello.

But most of all, she'd rekindled the fire of lust in his belly, and it burned and hurt like a live coal against his bare flesh.

Because it would never work. He could *never* get back what he'd lost.

How could he even want her so desperately, so physically, in so short a time? Was it because he'd been so barren, so isolated? And she was so incredibly alive? So interested in *him?*

Was it just the biochemical magic of human lust?

There was so little truly understood about the power of human chemistry. Of the electricity in a touch. Of the look in a woman's violet eyes.

He leaned his head back, cello still between his knees, and closed his eye, bringing her to mind. Her mouth. That little gap between her teeth. Those oasis eyes. Pale skin.

Tousled dark hair that made him think of bed-mussed mornings, the afterglow of making love.

And that small coal she'd ignited in him suddenly blazed hot inside his chest. While he was blaming Amelie for bringing him to life, while this was making him angry, while he was fighting it every step of the way even as he ached to taste more—he was losing sight of the real villain. The Moor. MagMo.

If there was one thing Tariq *could* still do with his life, and with these fires that were starting to rage inside him again, it was to help find The Moor, tear him and his terrorist empire down. He could still find a way to make his country safe for his family. For Omair's new baby. For Zakir's children—for their bloodline and future.

Even if he didn't have a future himself.

Bella booted up her computer and opened a Word file.

Outside the night was silent, snow falling softly again. On this side of the island there was no wind. Inside her room the oil heater popped and cracked as it warmed. She started to type:

> *Dr. Tariq Al Arif, next in line of succession to the Al Na'Jar throne and declared dead after a terrorist bombing at JFK ten months ago, has been found alive and living in France....*

She deleted the sentence, started again.

> *The prince of Al Na'Jar...*

She stalled, thinking of the way he'd struggled with the corkscrew, the way he walked so terrifyingly close to the cliff edge in darkness and fog, the haunted look in his features when he told her it was his fault the woman he loved died—the dark sensuality in his eyes as he'd watched her touching the puppy.

Tariq had no idea just how much she understood and knew about him.

She deleted her words, sat staring at the cursor blinking on the page, empathy welling in her chest.

He wasn't just some stranger to her. She'd covered his story so intimately she'd come to love the idea of him.

Could she do this now—expose him?

She *had* to. This was not just about exploiting his tragedy. This was her life, her job. Already people had died for this story. But how were they all linked—the Al Arif royals, The Moor and MagMo, the murders of Travis Johnson and his wife, Benjamin Raber, Sam Etherington?

A chill suddenly crawled over her skin as something struck her.

If The Moor and his MagMo insurgents were ultimately successful in overthrowing and taking control of Al Na'Jar, they'd take control of the considerable oil surplus there. Oil that Etherington was promising to a U.S. electorate should he become the next president. Could it mean Etherington's and MagMo's interests were aligned? She thought of the men who'd attacked her in D.C.—men who spoke Arabic. They'd come after her when she'd gone after Senator Etherington, looking for a link between him and the Al Arif royals.

She sat back in horror. That wasn't possible—was it? Sam Etherington in bed with a terrorist organization? No. He couldn't be. MagMo was beginning to rival Al Qaida in size and strength. The organization had been declared an enemy of the U.S.

Her computer beeped suddenly and Bella jolted in her chair. It was a call, coming from Hurley.

Quickly she clicked on the icon and Hurley's face filled the screen.

"Bella—we ran the biometrics. It's *him!* A one hundred percent match on all the images you sent. You have your proof. You have a story!"

She swallowed. The software Scoob used was military level. It would stand up to outside verification. She *could* run with this as is.

"What's the matter?" Hurley said, reading something in her face.

"It's not enough, Hurley. I need the rest—on STRIKE, on Etherington." She paused. "I met with him tonight."

"And?"

She bit her lip. "He's hurting."

Hurley frowned. "So? What about the story—did you get anything from him you can use?"

"I'm getting a tour of his abbey tomorrow. I hope to learn more then. Did you shred the photos?" she said.

"We did."

"And there's still no security breach?"

"Someone's still trying to hack in, bouncing like a bug against a lightbulb, but Scoob's keeping them at bay."

"Is he still looking into the Etherington-Raber connection?"

"Yeah, I'll call as soon as he gets something. And he thinks he might finally have found a way to clean up that audio from last summer. I'll let you know if he gets anything."

"Thanks, Hurley."

He paused, a strange look crossing his face.

"Bella—you *are* going to break this story on Watchdog, right?"

"Of course."

He was silent for several beats. "We've put a lot into this as well, you know."

"I know you have."

"Print media is a dinosaur, Bella. Citizen journalism—that's the future. Break this on the blog, finish what you started at the *Daily,* and the mainstream are going to come knocking on *our* doors. We're going to get hits. Agnes will be able to truly monetize the site. We'll be able—all of us—to draw a salary."

"Hurley, I'm *not* going anywhere else with this, relax. I promise."

His features relaxed a little. "I know how much you want to want to make a name, Bella—you're going to do it."

"I know," she said softly.

If I don't die first.

He signed off, his face fading with an electronic bloop.

Bella stared at her computer, pulse beating a little too fast. The temptation to go elsewhere with this was huge, and Hurley had sensed it. But she couldn't let the team down, not now. Not after everything they'd put into this.

Before shutting her computer off, Bella deleted her archives and Skype history, and she saved all her text documents onto a USB flash drive. She then wiped her computer clean of everything apart from her notes on the abbey and its ghost. Then she electronically shredded everything in her trash.

Removing the flash drive, she fastened it to the chain around her neck alongside the gold medallion. Flopping back onto her cot, she closed her eyes.

Tariq, dark, mysterious, filled her mind. She dozed off—and then he filled her dreams.

Bella woke with a start to banging on her door. Stumbling out of bed she punched her arms into her robe, gathering it about her waist as she opened her door to Estelle Dubois standing in the courtyard. Bella blinked against the light—the day had dawned impossibly bright, melting snow dripping from the wash line. Estelle's rheumy eyes gleamed, a grin creasing her powdery cheeks.

"Madame?"

"Out front," she said, breathless. "Monsieur Du Val, he has sent his limousine!"

"What?"

"Come, come," she beckoned with her arthritic hand as she shuffled quickly back through the courtyard to the main house.

Bella stuffed her feet into the bright green rubber clogs she kept by the door and followed Estelle Dubois into the living room, belting her robe as she went. Madame held back the drapes for Bella to peer through.

A black limo idled outside, exhaust fumes puffing white into the February air. Tariq's driver got out of the vehicle and began making his way up to the front door, his polished leather shoes slipping in the melting snow on the pathway.

Bella opened the door.

He dipped his head slightly. "Mademoiselle Chenard," he said. "Monsieur Du Val sent the car for you."

Another man appeared behind him, pushing her bike up the path, tires leaving a line in the snow. Her gaze went to the limo. They'd found a bike rack, or they'd bought one, because there had been no rack before.

She pushed her curls back off her face and glanced at the clock on the mantel. She'd overslept. How was that possible? She never overslept.

"Monsieur says there is another storm front blowing in. It will likely hit early this afternoon and will not be conducive to cycling. We are to bring you to the Abbaye Mont

Noir and return you once your tour is complete. Monsieur will conduct the tour himself."

Clutching her robe closed over her breasts, she said, "Himself? Why?"

"It's his wish."

Her heart started to hammer and she shot a look at Madame.

"Go." Madame waved her veined hand at Bella. "Have the day off. I need to rest. But you must take Kiki. She will disturb me—the older dog will leave me in peace." And with that she turned to shuffle into the kitchen, but Bella caught the smile on her lips. Madame was in her element as matchmaker.

"Can you wait maybe five minutes while I change and get my things together?" she asked the driver. "I'm running a bit late."

He dipped his head, studiously avoiding looking at her robe, her green clogs.

Bella showered so quickly the water didn't have time to warm properly. She pulled on her jeans, boots, sweater and coat, wrapping a scarf around her neck. She stuffed a woolen hat into a sling bag, along with her notebook and tape recorder. She grabbed her camera bag, caught a glimpse of herself in the mirror and stilled at her harried reflection. Ruffling her hair, she slicked on some lip gloss and ran out to the waiting car.

"Amelie!"

She stalled and spun round at the sound of Estelle Dubois' voice.

"You forgot Kiki!" She stood at the door, holding the pup and a ziplock bag of puppy kibble. "And don't forget to give her water."

Bella took the dog, and slipped the kibble into her bag.

Madame and Kiki had helped crack the ice last night—she was open to being helped out again.

Tariq stood at the abbey entrance watching his limousine snake up the twisting road, the gleaming black chrome like a hearse against the stark and blinding snow.

He inhaled deeply and stepped out from under the shadow of the portico into the sun as the vehicle neared the gates. Hooking his hands behind his back, he squared his shoulders, bracing to meet her.

He'd be lying if he didn't admit to a soft rush of anticipation. Whether he liked it or not, she was putting him back in the game. She was forcing him to think of his family, their safety, his country, and he was feeling like a prince again. A damaged one, but one with a role to play. Amelie had fanned the coals of a fire that had all but died in him—his desire to fight back.

To find and take down The Moor.

She might be innocent, and that was fine—he'd give her the tour and she'd be out of his life for good. But if she wasn't who she claimed to be, if Amelie was somehow linked to their enemy, he was going to use her to get that enemy.

There was also the chance she was some kind of reporter, seeking to expose him. Again, Omair would find this out. And somehow she'd have to be stopped, because right now The Moor likely believed Tariq and Omair were both dead. They wanted to keep it this way. It would lower The Moor's defenses, make him focus exclusively on Zakir and the kingdom where the royal army was strong and the kingdom had a firm contract with the F.D.S. for backup military support if necessary.

The limousine was nearing the gates, and worry fisted in his gut—Omair had not yet returned his call, and there'd been no answer when Tariq had tried again this morning. This was unusual for Omair. It also meant that for now, Tariq was on his own with Amelie, and his goal was to keep her close, see what more he and his men could learn themselves. It was also the reason he was conducting the tour personally today.

The iron gates swung slowly open and the vehicle tires crunched up the circular driveway, stopping in front of him. Sunlight glanced off the roof as the passenger door opened.

One booted leg swung out, but before Amelie could move any farther Tariq's man rushed around to hold the door open for her. She alighted, raven hair glinting with burgundy highlights in the sun. The little Papillon was tucked under one arm, a sling bag and camera bag clutched in her hand.

Her jeans were slim-fitting and showed her long legs to advantage. Her coat was open and underneath her sweater was striped and bright and body-hugging. Nothing about this woman was subtle. And unlike him, there was nothing she appeared to want to hide. She put Tariq in mind of a feisty polo pony with the kind of energy that could injure— or even kill—an experienced rider who wasn't careful.

He reminded himself to be careful.

But hot damn, he wanted to straddle and ride that energy, like he used to. All he could think about for a blinding instant was touching those pert breasts, peeling those snug layers of clothing off her body, feeling her skin, naked against his.

His heart started to slam hard against his rib cage.

She came up to him, features open, and she smiled warmly, showing that small gap between her teeth. In the stark sunlight Tariq could see a scattering of fine freckles over her nose and cheeks. He swallowed.

"Tahar," she said as she slung her bag over her shoulder and brushed delinquent curls back from her eyes. "I hear you'll be giving me the tour yourself. I'm thrilled, thank you."

Muscles strapped tight across his chest. "Where would you like to start?" His voice came out unnecessarily brusque.

She met his gaze and was silent for a beat, something shifting subtly in her features as she studied him. He wondered for an insane moment if she could read his mind. It made him hot under his clothes.

Under her scrutiny he also felt ugly in the broad daylight, exposed without his hood. Yet he *wanted* her to see him—all of him. Part of Tariq wanted to repel Amelie, unnerve her, even as he was attracted to her—or because he was.

But it wasn't working. He could detect no flinch in her features, no hesitation in her eyes. And on some level he knew his first move in this chess game was lost.

But the game was far from over.

Tariq turned his gaze toward his man standing beside the limo. The driver was still inside, engine still running. Tariq gave them a curt nod.

His bodyguard climbed back in, and the vehicle purred round the turning circle, the gates opening again as they headed back out.

Amelie followed his gaze. "Where are they going?"

"Abbey business."

She moistened her lips, something flashing through her eyes. Concern? But then she smiled again. "I was thinking from the top down," she said. "Are the battlements accessible? I read that the abbess used to walk up there daily, and that's where she likely saw the enemy ships coming over the horizon." Amelie looked up as she spoke, taking in the huge Catherine window above the arched doors. The sun was catching the stained glass, making it glow as if internally lit.

"Wow," she whispered.

Something akin to pride flushed through Tariq, which shocked him a little. He'd actually forgotten the beauty he'd first seen hidden in the abbey. He felt himself stand a little taller.

"The stairs to the battlements are not in very good condition," he said. "That part of the abbey has not yet been refurbished."

"We could go carefully."

He inhaled. "This way," he said, holding his hand out toward the hallway.

He caught her scent as she passed close by. Soapy, clean. No perfume today. His butler took her coat and tension torqued painfully through Tariq's body as he followed Amelie through the hallway, noting the way her jeans hugged the curves of her behind like a second skin. Keeping her close was definitely going to come with collateral damage. To him. It already had. It was now up to him to control how much. Because on some level Tariq knew he could still stop this physical attraction—and that he didn't quite want to.

Opening a heavy door at the end of a passageway, he said, "The stairs go up this way. Be careful, they're crumbling in places and there is no light other than what comes in through the murder holes."

"The what?"

"Gaps for arrows. The building was always used as a monastery," he explained. "But it was constructed with defense in mind." He held his hand out to the spiral stairwell that curled up the spire.

She entered the stairwell ahead of him, dog still in her

arms. Tariq stole a quick glance at his watch, getting increasingly worried about Omair and Faith now. He'd left his satellite phone with one of his men with instructions to summon him the minute Omair phoned.

He began to climb after her, leaning one hand occasionally against the rough circular wall to support his injured leg. He tried not to watch her rear, or notice how slender her waist was. Or imagine how her body might feel under his. But God help him, he couldn't concentrate on anything but. His breathing grew heavy as the stairwell wound tighter, darker, higher. He stopped, closing his eyes for a very brief moment, biting back pain. As he did, anger mushroomed through him. Denial, he thought. He was still in denial—he still could not accept his physical limitations, his loss. And he wanted revenge.

Was desiring Amelie in his bed part of that hunger for revenge? A way of angrily thrusting back, just to lash out, prove he was still human, still male? Or was it another way of trying to bury his pain and emotions as he might bury himself blindly in her flesh?

Whatever it was, he couldn't do it. He must not touch her. For so many reasons.

By the time they reached the top and stepped out through an archway into a burst of bright light, Tariq was thankful for the lungful of fresh, chilly air. He drunk it deep into his lungs, clearing the errant thoughts from his head.

From up here they could see for miles, and in the distance a bank of bad weather was building on the horizon and beginning to roll over the Atlantic toward the island—the next storm front would be on them by this afternoon.

Amelie set the little puppy down and it scampered over rock and moss to sniff along the parapet. She turned in a slow circle, taking in the deep emerald moss, the lichens blooming in shades of ochre and cream on the ancient stone battlements. Then she went to the wall and faced the sea, staring out at the lighthouse on a distant lump of rock. Far below, the Atlantic heaved and was streaked with ribs of white foam. He could taste the salt in the crisp breeze. He watched the way the wind ruffled her hair and pinked her cheeks.

"The abbess would have stood here, watching." Amelie almost whispered the words as she placed her palms flat on the stone wall. Tariq wondered if in her mind's eye she was picturing ancient enemy sails cresting the horizon, if she was imagining the abbess's terror at the sight of a medieval army approaching.

She began to walk along the parapet, trailing her fingers over stone as she continued to gaze out over the water. He walked just behind her.

"Watch your step," he said suddenly, shooting out his hand to indicate the uneven surface at her feet. But it was too late—distracted by the view Amelie snagged the toe of her boot and stumbled wildly forward.

He lunged for her, catching her and taking her weight with his crippled left arm. She grabbed hold of his maimed hand.

He could feel her breast press against his arm, the rapid beating of her pulse at her wrist.

"Thanks. I didn't even see that," she said, a little breathless. She straightened up, but remained close, her gaze traveling to the claw she held so tightly. She swallowed, then looked back up into his eye, and a strange sort of power surged through Tariq when she didn't pull away. He'd caught her with his disfigured side—and she wasn't repulsed by it. He'd found a strength he didn't knew he had.

With that notion came a wash of affection. It was such a human thing, to be accepted, to not be shunned.

Then he saw arousal in her eyes, the way her mouth was slightly open. Blood began to pound in his ears, narrowing his world. Not only was she accepting him for what he was now, she wanted him—as he wanted her.

Very slowly she reached up, lightly touching the injured side of his face. Inside Tariq flinched instinctively—his scars, his wounds, had not been touched by a woman in this way. But he did not break her gaze, did not pull away.

Her fingertips gently traced the scar down the side of his face, lower, lower to where it pulled down his lips. The sensation was distant, his nerves there too damaged, but lust arrowed like a spear of molten lead into his groin. And Tariq was suddenly incapable of pulling away. Incapable of stopping feelings he thought he might still be able to control. Perspiration began to prickle over his torso. He could hear the waves crunch and suck on the rocks below, and he breathed in the scent of moss and salt. And her.

More than anything, at this moment, suspended in time and history among these ancient stones, he wanted to grab hold of her, pull her hard up against his chest, crush her mouth under his own.

"I'm glad you're not wearing your hood, Tahar," Bella whispered. She saw him swallow, hard, and it excited her to see the dark arousal in his features, the glittering awareness in his black eye. His desire for her. It scared her a little, too, the intensity in him.

She'd never gone for the ordinary—and this man was everything but. Yet it was more than lust that welled hot in her chest now—it was a desire to heal, to ease his pain, to hold, comfort. To share. To just be herself with him—tell him who she was. Bella realized she wanted Tariq to like her, the *real* her. And on some level she realized that this was no longer just a story. Maybe it was never just a story.

Maybe it was always about her feelings for this man.

His eye patch was silky in this light, and his good eye, fringed by the thickest, blackest lashes she'd ever seen, smoldered with something so dark it burned inside her. The unforgiving sunlight hid nothing—yet everything about him remained hidden, simmering, just below the surface.

Time seemed to stretch, quiver. Then several more beats of silence turned things awkward, and he abruptly pulled back. Dragging her hand through her hair, she turned away to hide the flush of embarrassment she could feel coloring her cheeks and she began to make an exaggerated fuss of getting her camera out of her bag.

"Do you mind?" she said, holding up the camera, her voice all business.

His features had turned hard, guarded again.

"Have you already downloaded what's in there?" he said cooly.

"No," she lied. Then nervousness made her way, "Why?"

A small muscle began to tick at his jaw. "You can take whatever photos you like of the abbey, Amelie, but before you do, I need you to delete whatever images you have in there."

She stared at him. "Are you serious?"

"Dead serious."

A movement suddenly caught her eye and Bella glanced toward the archway that led to the stairs. One of his men stood there now, in shadow, his broad body blocking the exit. A tiny tongue of fear flicked through her. She hadn't even realized they'd been followed.

"The photos you took of me on the cliff," he said quietly. "I'd like them deleted."

"I…I won't use them for anything. I'm just keeping them for…atmosphere. For my novel."

His face darkened. His bodyguard moved slightly forward.

"These are my conditions, Amelie. Delete the photographs, or I'll have my men do it for you."

Fear flicked harder. She glanced again at his guard. And Bella realized she'd let her own defenses drop too far. He'd been playing her all along.

Chapter 5

Bella felt hot spots of anger form high on her cheeks.

"So *that's* why you invited me back with my camera, so you could take your photos? Is that also why you decided to show me around yourself?"

"My privacy is everything, Amelie," he said quietly. "If you're being truthful about why you're here, you'll understand—you don't need those images of me."

She stared him, mind racing.

Be careful, Bella—he's testing you.

"What did you think I was going to do with them, anyway—put them up on the internet?"

"I can't take that risk."

"Why is it so damn important for you to hide, Tahar?"

He studied her, silent for several beats. "I need the time. I need to heal."

"Or maybe you don't want the people who care about you to discover you walk too close to the cliffs every night," she said.

His features turned dangerous, an energy, palpable, rolling off him in waves.

"It's as if you stand on that cliff edge waiting for the ground to give way under your feet, for gravity and nature to make a decision you don't have the guts to make yourself."

The muscles in his neck corded. But he refused to take the bait. Instead, voice cool, he said, "Are you *sure* you haven't downloaded the photos into your computer?"

"Yes, I'm sure," she said curtly.

And it struck Bella suddenly—the way Tariq had nodded to his men before they'd left in the limo. Had he sent them back to check her computer for the photos? Was he playing her on an even deeper level than she'd first realized? Her pulse started to race wildly.

It was okay, she told herself. There was nothing to find in her laptop—she'd deleted and shredded anything incriminating. All her files, including the photos of him, were now stored in the flash drive on a chain nestled between her breasts under her sweater. But a new wave of panic crashed afresh through Bella—her passport, ID, credit card were in her room. She'd hidden them in a cavity under a loose floorboard like in too many bad spy movies, but there'd been nowhere else.

"Fine." She held out the camera, praying they wouldn't find her documents, because it was becoming crystal clear that this man did not trust her at all, even as he was attracted to her, and he was not going to take proof of her deception lightly. "Delete them yourself," she said.

Tariq motioned to his guard who came forward and took her camera. He fiddled with it, killing files, then handed it back to Bella.

"Gee, thanks," she said sarcastically.

"I hope you understand," Tariq said.

Oh, she understood all right—he didn't want anyone to know the prince of Al Na'Jar was alive. That his death was an elaborate lie. She'd do the same in his position.

"I'm not sure that I do," she lied.

"Do you want to continue with the tour—or leave it here?"

Bella blew air out of her lungs. "Continue. Do you mind if I take pictures now?"

"Fair enough, but only of the abbey, no people."

She got busy, shooting images of the battlements, the bank of dark gray fog crawling ever closer over the Atlantic swells. Already the lighthouse in the distance had been swallowed by it, and she could feel a new dampness in the air, a sharp drop in temperature. She wondered about the ghost again as she crouched down to snap some close-ups of the mosses and lichens growing on the ancient rock. Her gaze was then pulled upward to the crumbling turrets and spires. She could feel Tariq watching her closely, too closely, feel his bodyguard's scrutiny from the shadows.

"Is that where the wind screams?" she said, nodding at the turrets.

"Yes," he said curtly. Whatever undercurrent that had passed between them earlier was gone.

Bella got to her feet and went to the other side of the wall. From here she could see back into the abbey grounds, and in the distance, the ruins of a chapel, a graveyard with tumbling headstones. Creepers grew up the inner walls that were protected from the salty sea winds. And along the one wing was a walled-off garden. A man in a white chef's jacket carrying a basket was picking what appeared to be herbs and vegetables. A kitchen garden, thought Bella.

Again, the sensation of having stepped back in time washed over her.

"Seen enough up here?" His voice broke into her thoughts.

She nodded.

He held out his hand toward the stairwell, careful this time to keep his distance from her. Bella glanced over her shoulder. The bodyguard had seemingly vanished. Perhaps he was watching from somewhere else. She whistled for Kiki and the little dog came running, lichen stuck on its nose. Bella picked up the pup, brushed the brown stuff off its muzzle and started down the stairs, twisting round and round as she spiraled down, conflict coiling tighter and tighter inside her. Through the murder holes she caught glimpses of the smoke-gray wall of weather almost upon them.

Back downstairs Bella excused herself to go to the washroom. She needed a moment to gather her thoughts, to contact Estelle Dubois to find out if Tariq's men had been there.

Tariq took the dog from her and told her he'd be waiting in the pool room. He said his butler would show her to the pool when she was done.

Bella watched the prince walk away, Madame's little dog in his arms. His limp had worsened after climbing the stairs. A strange conflict curled through her chest—a potent cocktail of desire and fear, empathy and affection, and exhilaration at the idea of breaking this story, of finding out more. More than ever she needed to stay focused, keep her wits about her. There was no one else to watch out for her. Misstep now, in this monastery, behind these spiked walls, and she'd be at his mercy.

The bathroom was beautiful—a vase of fresh white flowers graced the sink, green-and-white Grecian-style tiles. Big mirrors. It spoke of a woman's touch, and Bella wondered if this portion of the abbey had been renovated while Julie was still alive. The thought sobered her as she leaned forward and splashed water on her face. She stared at herself in the mirror, thinking of Tariq's touch, the look in his eye. The electricity that had crackled between them. There was no doubt in her mind that Tariq was physically attracted to her, but at the same time she'd glimpsed something akin to hatred in his features, although he'd quickly hid it. Tariq was at war inside himself over her, and she suspected one reason was Julie, and his loyalty to her memory.

Why was she doing this to him?

Focus, Bella. You know why.

This wasn't just about her job, or proving herself anymore—people had died trying to tip her off for this story. She had an obligation to see this through, on several fronts.

Taking her cell phone from her bag, Bella punched in Madame's number. She wanted to ask Estelle Dubois if Tariq's men had returned, and to check that the door to her room was properly locked. But there was no answer. Estelle had probably turned the ringer off as was her usual practice when she took a nap. Cursing softly, Bella pocketed the phone.

Outside the bathroom the butler was waiting discreetly.

"This way," he said, ushering her down a hall, the faint scent of chlorine entering the air as they neared the pool room.

Bella entered the large room and stilled in awe. A long black pool glistened before her, the water seeming to flow under the floor-to-ceiling windows and vanish over the cliff edge outside. Steam rose from a whirlpool built into one end of the pool, and beyond the whirlpool, behind a thick wall of smoked glass, was a gym full of gleaming chrome equipment.

Turning in a half circle, she searched for Tariq and finally saw him crouched awkwardly at the far end of the room near an indoor garden feature, playing with the dog, ruffling its fur. She smiled, cleared her throat.

Startled, he looked up.

His features shuttered as Bella approached, and he struggled quickly to his feet, a sharp flash of pain across his face as he did. Then came an arrogant forward thrust of his jaw, as if he was furious for revealing weakness.

Kiki was immune to it all, hopping about his boots for more attention.

"You have an affinity for animals," she said as she came up to him, thinking of the way he rode polo ponies, the saluki hounds his family had always hunted with.

He gave a snort. "Ready to see the rest of the abbey?"

"Absolutely. This has to be one of the most stunning pool and gym setups I've ever seen. Do you use it often?" she said, nodding to the water.

"I did last night."

"What about the gym?"

"Fired my physical therpist on day one."

She crooked a brow. "How come?"

"Didn't need her around, waste of her time."

She studied him quietly for several beats. "You don't really want to get better, do you, Tahar?" she said softly.

His face darkened. "Better? Look at this." He held out his crippled left hand. "*This* is fact. This is not going to get better. I was a surgeon, Amelie. I will never operate again."

She swallowed at the rawness in his voice, the truth. "I…I'm so sorry."

Tariq turned his back on Amelie, began striding toward the door, his shoulders tight, sparks of pain shooting through his hip and neck. This woman was pushing him to the edge, a much more dangerous one from the cliff face he walked daily.

"Tahar!" she called after him.

He stopped, but refused to turn to face her.

"I *am* sorry. I don't know what else to say!"

"There is nothing to say. I don't want your sympathy. I don't want people saying they're sorry, looking at me like I'm some goddamn broken thing. What I want is for you to take what you need and leave me the hell alone."

Bella took a step closer. "You're self-indulgent, you know that? Full of self-pity. *You're* the one who just pointed out to me that you were broken, that you would never operate again. But you *can* still use your medical skills for other things. You're *alive,* Tahar. *You* didn't die in that accident!"

His fists clenched.

"Everything I care about did," Tariq said quietly. Then he made briskly for the door, calling out over his shoulder as he went, "You want to see dungeons, I'll show you dungeons."

Anger pounded through his chest as he reached the door. She didn't know the half of his accident.

And her words stung like all hell.

Because he saw the truth in them. And in this moment he hated her for that truth. He wanted this tour over, wanted her gone, *now.* But as he stepped through the pool room door, his butler appeared with his sat phone in hand.

"You have a call, sir."

Tariq reached for the phone, checked the incoming number. Omair.

"I'll take this in my study," he said to his butler in French. Then he turned to Bella. "I need to take a call. Wait here."

"I… Sure."

Tariq entered his office and shut the heavy wooden door firmly behind him. Once he'd spoken to Omair, once his brother's people started digging, he'd know everything he needed to know about Amelie Chenard. And if she was toying with him, she was going to regret it.

"Omair," he said into the phone. "How are you—how is Faith, the baby?" Then before Omair could answer, Tariq said, "Is that him I can hear crying?"

"It is," said Omair with a laugh, the sound so deep and rich Tariq was instantly overwhelmed by emotion. There was nothing in the world quite like the sound of a newborn baby's cry. He was silent for a moment, his throat tight as he clutched the phone. He missed his brother suddenly, his family. He should be there—he should meet his new nephew. His isolation felt wrong.

He needed to find a way to come back to life and rejoin them.

Amelie had done this to him. As much as he resented her presence, as much as he was fighting his physical attraction to her, she'd made him reach out to his brother, his family. For their help.

"He's a little terror," Omair said. "He's been giving Faith and me a run for our money, far worse than any mission either of us has been on."

Tariq felt himself smile, the movement foreign and pulling against his scars. "Bring the phone closer to him, Omair," he said. "I want to listen to him."

Tariq listened to the sound of his brother's newborn son crying. It sent chills through his body. His thoughts turned to Zakir, to Nikki, and their seven-month-old twins. Tariq swallowed against the ball of emotion swelling bigger in his throat.

"Did you hear?" Omair said. "His name is Adam, Tariq. You should use his name."

"Adam," he said quietly. He knew what Omair was doing—making him real for Tariq, trying to make him feel things, to bring him to life again. His family had been so worried about him, and Amelie was right—he'd been self-absorbed, selfish in his grief.

"I did hear him. He sounds like he will be trouble, like his father. Is Faith getting much sleep?"

"Sleep is a long-lost friend," Omair said, "for both of us. But Dalilah will be arriving next week. She's coming to help out, give Faith a chance to rest while I get back to some work." He chuckled again.

"Dalilah is coming?"

"Couldn't keep her away." Omair paused, his voice changing. "It's safer that she doesn't return to New York right now. At least until we know who and what we're up against. The F.D.S. will be flying her in from Al Na'Jar."

Thoughts of his colorful, exotically beautiful sister filled Tariq's mind. He hadn't been truly thinking of her safety. Remorse was bitter in his mouth, self-recrimination burned.

Amelie was wrong.

He *did* want to get better.

He just didn't know how, because he was not the same man and never would be. His neurosurgery skills had come to define him. Medicine—healing—was his passion. That had been taken from him. And his dream of having his own family with Julie been dashed like the waves that crashed onto rocks at the base of the cliffs on this island.

Tariq reminded himself he was still a prince. He still had two of his brothers and his sister. They still had their kingdom. The Moor had not taken those things from them—not yet.

And now, there were the new nieces and a nephew, Al Arif blood in their veins.

Tariq's hand tightened around the phone, and he squared his shoulders. For these things he would fight. He would protect.

"And how are *you,* brother?" Omair was saying.

"I'm fine. I've got more mobility—been using the pool. Might try the gym next. But another issue has come up and I need your help." Tariq went to his desk and clicked his computer to life as he spoke.

"There's a woman on the island, an American, who has a very keen interest in the abbey. She also tried to take photos of me out on the heath, and she ambushed me in a restaurant. She claims she's doing research for a novel that she wants to set on the island, and she's asked for a tour of the place. I don't trust her. I need you to get your people to run a deep background check."

Omair was quiet for a moment, and when he spoke again, Tariq heard the shift in his tone.

"What information can you give me?"

Bella went to the big windows that yawned from floor to ceiling, and she watched the dark fog wall swallowing the landscape, wisps of mist fingering up the cliff, crawling over the pearly black water outside, closing a fist around the monastery walls. She rubbed her arms, a strange shiver chasing over her skin. Then she heard a yip and jerked around, startled.

The pool room door from which Tariq had exited was partially ajar, and Kiki was scratching at it, trying to widen the gap. Bella cursed—she'd all but forgotten the dog.

"No, Kiki," she called. "Over here!"

But Kiki wiggled through the gap, pushing the door open wide with her body. She sniffed the stone tiles where Tariq had stood. And like a shot she was off after him, tracking him down the passage.

"Kiki, get back here, now!" Bella ran after the dog.

The little animal vanished around a corner at the end of

the dim passage. "Kiki!" Bella called, hustling round the corner just in time to see Kiki disappearing into the library.

She cursed again, and ran lightly down the passage to the library. Edging the heavy wood door open she saw the room was empty. Again, a fire crackled in the hearth, filling the room with a warmth and ambience absent in the rest of the abbey. Persian rugs felt plush underfoot. Kiki was on the far end of the room snuffling under the closed door to Tariq's study.

"Come here, you little terror," she whispered as she hurriedly crossed the soft carpets. She bent down to pick up the dog, and stilled as she heard the sonorous tone of Tariq's voice behind the door. His voice rose suddenly in what sounded like anger, and she realized with a jolt he was speaking Arabic.

Slowly, she stood up, dog in one arm. On the table, right beside the study door, where his jacket hung over the back of a chair, was his wallet.

Bella shot a quick glance toward the door that opened out into the passage, then she inched over to the table. Heart in throat, she reached out, flipped open the book wallet. She threw another glance at the door, then returned her attention to the wallet, looking for ID, anything that might add proof and weight to her story even if he chose not to comment. Because that was beginning to look slim right now.

There was cash inside. But no credit cards or driver's license. She flipped to the next compartment. Two photographs were tucked behind plastic. One was of Julie Belard, elegant, polished, groomed. Even her smile was sophisticated—a woman fit to marry an oil-rich sheik, to become a royal princess. Unlike Bella DiCaprio from Chicago, no real job, no idea where she really came from.

On the opposite side of the wallet was a photo of the

royal family. Bella's gaze shot back to his office door.
Tariq was still talking. Kiki squirmed under her arm as
she edged the wallet closer. She bent over to scrutinize
the image of King Zakir, Tariq, Omair, their sister Dalilah
and—Bella's breath caught in her throat—*Queen Nikki Al
Arif without her veil.*

The queen had never been photographed or seen in public without a veil. Her pulse raced as she studied the image
of the mysterious woman said to hail from Norway. She
truly was beautiful: classic features, wide eyes, full mouth,
thick honey-blond hair. Something began to buzz inside
Bella's head. The queen looked disturbingly familiar—
Bella could swear she'd seen a picture of this woman before, and recently. But where?

Tariq stilled, his hand tightening on the phone as he
thought he heard a sound outside his door.

"Hold on," he quietly told Omair. He listened intently,
but there was nothing more. Reaching for his mouse, he
copied the links to Amelie's website and social media page
into an email. He added Omair's address, clicked Send.

"I'm forwarding you some links with photographs and
other information. Her name is Amelie Chenard, speaks
excellent French. She has a website and some social media
presence. It all looks fairly recent, but that could be because of previous ghostwriting contractual obligations to
secrecy."

"You think she could be connected to MagMo?"
Omair said.

"If she came here to kill me she would have done so
already. She had a perfect opportunity out on the heath,
just before dark. And if she was a reporter looking to find
me alive, she would have run a story already—she took

photographs of my face, used a big telephoto lens. But I've scoured the internet and nothing has come up."

"Do you have the photos she took?"

"They've been deleted," Tariq said. "My men are searching her room and computer as we speak to ensure there's nothing that could be used." Tariq ran his hand over his hair. "She might be exactly who she claims, Omair, but we need to be sure."

A beat of silence, then Omair said, "We?"

Tariq huffed.

Omair chuckled dryly. "She might be dangerous, brother, but clearly she's got the old fire burning in you again. I'll get my men on this. Meanwhile, keep her close— I can't stress this enough. Watch her carefully until we've done the full background check."

A movement sounded behind the study door. Tariq's voice rose again—he was signing off. Bella's heart jumped into her throat. Hurriedly, she removed the photograph from the plastic and slipped it into the back pocket of her jeans. She flipped the wallet closed and started to tiptoe rapidly across the carpet, but she heard the door handle behind her creak.

She wasn't going to make it!

Bella veered sharply to her right, heading for the bookshelves. Just as the door opened, she bent down as if examining titles on a lower shelf, the dog clutched too tightly in her arm.

"Oh, hi," she said, straightening up, perspiration pricking her body. "Kiki trailed you from the pool room. I had to run after her, and then I got distracted by your books."

A strange look crossed his face. He glanced back into his study, and she could see him wondering if she'd heard him on the phone.

Bella tried to swallow against the dryness in her mouth. "Is everything okay? Did you get bad news?"

"I'll know soon enough whether the news is bad," he said darkly.

Bella turned her face away from him, worried he could read guilt in her features. She trailed her fingers over the spines of his books, moving down the row of shelves as she pretended to casually peruse titles, her heart thumping.

If he saw the photo was missing from his wallet he'd know right away it was her. She shouldn't have taken it, but she was convinced she'd seen the queen's face somewhere, and recently. Her impulse had been to snatch it so she could look again, closely. Now she was stuck.

Bella could feel his gaze boring into her and his silence was heavy. Her body began to get hot. Why wasn't he speaking? Did he know something? Was he testing her?

She tried to focus on the titles. "You've got a whole shelf here devoted to absurdist and existentialist philosophers and novelists," she said, angling her head to read the authors' names, Kiki squirming in her arm. "Jean-Paul Sartre, Søren Kierkegaard, Franz Kafka, Fyodor Dostoyevsky, Jean Améry." She stopped at the Améry title, removed the book from the shelf: *On Suicide: A Discourse on Voluntary Death*.

She glanced up at him and tension balled in her stomach at the look on his face.

"Améry survived Auschwitz and Buchenwald," she said quietly, but she was shaking inside. "And after all that, he killed himself in '78. He used pills."

"You know your Améry."

She was silent for a beat. "I studied literature, remember? Philosophy, too."

He came closer, the energy rolling off him dark, crackling. "Améry saw the ability to take his own life as the ultimate freedom from humanity," he said.

"Should it be one's goal, to be free of one's humanity?"

"Have you never wished—" he replied, voice low, sensual, a little threatening "—to escape the absurdity of life?"

She laughed lightly, but it sounded hollow even to her own ears. "God, no."

The image of him in his cloak on the cliff edge swirled like cool mist into her mind. She wondered if he had some kind of post-traumatic stress from the bombing, if his family knew this, or even if he recognized it in himself. And just didn't care.

Bella's attention went to the book beside his chair, a bookmark poking out of it. He'd been reading Camus's *La Mort Heureuse*. A Happy Death.

He really was struggling to live.

Perhaps it wasn't just P.T.S.D. Brain injuries could also induce depression, change personality.

She might be the only one who could really see what was happening to him, who knew what he'd been before, and could see now how very close to the edge he was walking. The responsibility suddenly weighed heavy on Bella's shoulders. Lying to him, exposing him felt wrong. Stealing his photo was wrong.

But she also had an obligation to follow her story to the end—it could be in national interests. She couldn't forget Althea Winston, who'd died to tip her off. And Bella had a duty to herself, too. She had to earn a living. No one else was going to look after her.

Conflict tightened in her chest.

"Did your accident happen in France?" she said quietly, the Améry book still in her hand, Kiki squirming under her other arm.

His brow lowered. "Why?"

Bella replaced the book on the shelf. "Just wondering—you seem foreign." Her eyes trailed to the higher shelves. "And you have some Arabic titles up there."

"I read many languages."

Slowly she turned to face him. "Tahar, maybe you shouldn't…" She trailed off, suddenly unable to hold his burning gaze. Instead she set Kiki back onto the floor. The little dog squiggled excitedly at his feet, but he ignored the animal, kept his eye on her.

"Shouldn't what?" he said.

"I was going to say maybe you shouldn't be so alone. Maybe you need friends, family. Do you have family?"

Suspicion coiled in Tariq's gut and it swirled with desire he couldn't shake when he was this close to her. And that made him angry—the fact he wasn't in control, that she had this power over him. The temptation to throw her out at once thrummed through his body, the fire inside him building to almost irrational proportions. His chest began to burn, the beat of his blood loud against his eardrums, the whole library blurring in the periphery of his mind as he focused on her. He could hear Omair's words.

Keep her close. Watch her carefully until we've done the full background check.

"I know I'm making you angry," Amelie said quietly, her cheeks flushed. "But I suspect that's because anger is the easiest emotion for you—it's the only emotion you will allow yourself because it helps block out the pain."

She was right. It was easier than feeling pain. Or lust. Holding on to rage was a way of holding on to the past, the memory of Julie, of not having to face a new future and properly deal with his disabilities. His anger began to vibrate inside.

"Let's get the tour over with," he said brusquely, brushing past her and making swiftly for the door.

But as he stalked into the cold stone corridor all he could think about was crushing her in his arms, feeling her lips under his as he kissed her angrily, passionately, fiercely. If she didn't leave soon, something inside him was going to blow.

Chapter 6

Bella followed Tariq as he stalked down the passage, Kiki's tiny nails clicking on stone behind her. She wished she'd brought a leash.

"The abbey renovations stopped here," Tariq said as they entered a wide walkway spaced with tall gothic arches that opened to a courtyard of grass gone long and shrubs gone wild. The air out here was cool, damp, with mist blowing in through the stone openings.

"This walkway connects the other wings of the abbey. The east wing, over there, includes what were once sleeping quarters for the monastic inhabitants. Across the courtyard over there—" He pointed. "You can see the ruins of the chapel, and beside it, the old cemetery." His voice was deadpan, but his neck muscles were corded with tension, and a dark kinetic energy emanated from him in waves. He met her gaze for a moment, held.

Bella swallowed at what she saw there.

She averted her eyes, and busied herself clicking several photos through one of the arches, focusing first on the crumbling spire of the chapel, then the crucifix on top, the tumbling walls being devoured by creepers.

"The dungeons are this way." He began walking.

Bella called Kiki and hurried to catch up with him. At the dungeon entrance, one of Tariq's bodyguards waited with flashlights in hand.

"Why did you stop the refurbishing?" she asked as they approached the guard.

"I lost interest."

"Because of the accident?"

He didn't reply.

"It's because she's gone, isn't it—your fiancée? You said you bought this place for her but now it means nothing because she's not here."

He whirled round, daggers in his eye, energy sparking off him.

Bella stalled, her breath snaring in her chest. She was pushing all his buttons and she knew it—she was hoping he'd snap, reveal some truth, give her an opening to tell him why he'd really invited her here. But she was also afraid of him now.

"Understand this, Amelie," he said, voice low, cool. "I'm obliging your research. That's all. And your research has nothing to do with me."

"How long has it been, Tahar?" she whispered, pushing. "Since the accident."

He glowered at her. Time stretched.

"Ten months," he said finally.

She opened her mouth, surprised, again, by him telling the truth, but he stopped her abruptly with the palm of his hand. "Don't," he said. "Do not even try to say a thing. You wanted a tour—then let's get the damn thing over with."

He started to walk again. "This is where the ghost of the abbess has supposedly been sighted most often," he said, indicating the arches.

"Before I bought the place people used to come in through gaps in the property wall behind the cemetery to watch for the ghost. They claim that in a certain slant of moonlight her silhouette can be seen moving from archway to archway. Legend has it that her spirit comes up from the dungeons where her body is trapped, and she moves along this walkway trying to get up to the battlements. They say she stands up there sometimes and watches a moonlit sea. And when the storms blow in, as you already know, you can allegedly hear her screams."

Goose bumps prickled over Bella's skin. The air was markedly cooler as they neared the dark, dungeon entrance.

Tariq's bodyguard stepped forward. He gave his boss a flashlight, then handed one to Bella. She noted he kept the third for himself, and wondered if he would follow them, or wait up here in case he was called down.

"Leave the puppy with him," Tariq said crisply. "It's dark down there, lots of places to lose a little dog."

Reluctantly, she scooped up Kiki and placed the little dog in the huge bodyguard's arms. His face was impassive, his eyes unreadable. Nervousness chased through Bella. She glanced at Tariq. "Madame Dubois will fire me, or worse, if something happens to that dog. I need my job."

"Take the dog to the kitchen," he said to his man.

"Kitchen?" Bella said.

"There's an enclosed herb garden off the kitchen," Tariq said. "There's also food and water, and it's a warm place to sleep. The chef likes animals." He paused, something in his features softening almost imperceptibly. "Puppies get tired, you know. And hungry and thirsty. Kiki will be fine."

"I…thank you. I've never had pets."

"I've had plenty. Dogs, horses, birds." He clicked on his flashlight, entered the dark archway.

Bella switched on her own beam of light and followed. She was getting closer and closer with his truths—she knew of his polo ponies, his hunting horses, his falcons. And he'd been unable to hide his tenderness for Kiki.

The air that seeped up the stairwell as they descended was heavy with the musty scent of age and moisture.

As they went deeper, the mustiness felt thick in her nostrils, the walls seemed to narrow in on them. The darkness pushing against their yellow beams grew so complete it felt tangible, sentient.

Uneasy, Bella panned her flashlight around. Shadows leaped and quivered as she moved. Her heart beat faster. She tried to stay close to Tariq. His black hair gleamed in the glow of her flashlight.

Lower down she heard dripping. Suddenly the air felt like pure ice.

At the bottom of the stairs he turned, waited for her. In the quavering shadows his face, his scars, his eye patch, looked threatening. Fear closed a noose around her neck—if she disappeared down here no one would ever find her. Bella told herself she was being ridiculous, but she could almost feel the weight of the monastery pressing down on her, and a wave of claustrophobia licked through her chest. She hated the idea of being trapped down here, hated thinking about the abbess's bones behind one of these rock walls. Hated her sudden, irrational fear of this man, even as she was attracted to him.

"This way." He touched her elbow, and she started, heart jackhammering. But all he wanted to do was guide her through what appeared to be a row between cells, the stone beneath their feet uneven and potholed. He shone his beam into one of the cells. Rusting shackles hung from chains embedded in the rock. The scent of mold, and something worse, was thick.

"If you've done your reading," he said, "you'll know about the prisoners that were brought down here during the rebellion."

She swallowed, hugging even closer to him as he moved farther along the row. Air currents shifted around them, as if something was in the cold, dank shadows, watching, waiting, touching. She shivered.

"I can't imagine the horror of being imprisoned down here," she whispered.

"Some were left until they died."

Bella panned her light into another cell as she passed. A rusted iron door hung open, bars across a tiny window in the door. She could almost feel terror in the dank air, hear screams. See whites of terrified eyes, smell rotten teeth, broken limbs, urine. For a moment she couldn't move.

Tariq felt a shift in Amelie and turned. Her face was sheet white in the beam of his light.

"Are you all right?"

"Yeah, yes, I...I'm fine." But her eyes were wide.

"We can go back up—"

"No." She touched his arm, and he tensed. "I need to see where the abbess's body was walled in. Please."

He glanced down at her hand on his arm, then gently, he took her by the elbow again. "Come, it's at the end of this row of cells."

Tariq liked the feel of Amelie against him, the way she was staying close. Too close. It made his mouth dry.

"How big is this dungeon area? How many rows like this?"

"It's vast. A maze, and much of it in bad repair. You wouldn't want to be lost down here without a light. Too easy to fall and get hurt."

She held on to his arm tightly now, steadying herself as they stepped over crumbling rock. It gave Tariq a soft rush of power, to be needed, even just a little. Part of what he liked about being a doctor was being needed by people, and being able to help allay their fears, heal them. It gave him control. And having control over life made him feel alive. Valued. He realized just how much he'd lost that sense of virility after failing Julie—after having her die in his arms. And how Amelie was somehow infusing him with a sense of purpose again.

He stopped at the wall of wet, black stone.

"This is it," he said to Amelie. "The abbess's bones are supposed to be behind this wall."

She gave a soft little intake of breath and bumped against him.

"What is it?" he said.

"I thought I felt…it's nothing."

He'd felt it, too—a presence, a sense of being watched. But for a moment Tariq couldn't think beyond the firm softness of her breast pressing against his arm. And a need so fundamentally raw flooded through Tariq—an urge to gather her close, hold her tightly against his broken body, draw from her vitality, her warmth. To feel real—to make love again.

When he spoke again his voice came out thick. "She was apparently beheaded down here, her headless body tossed into this last cell before it was walled in with stone."

Amelie panned the beam of her flashlight over the glistening rock wall. "And they stuck her head on a spike outside the main gate, all because she was harboring a fugitive?"

"A revolutionary," he said. "Some claim he was her lover."

She glanced up, met his gaze. Air stirred between them,

like icicles touching his skin. Amelie shivered, obviously feeling it, too.

"You think her bones are really in there?"

"I have no reason not to believe it."

"And you haven't thought of opening this wall up, checking? Maybe exhuming her remains?"

"Why?" he said quietly.

Surprise showed in her eyes. "I hate the idea of anyone being trapped down here. All this cold stone weighing down over your head, the darkness, the damp, the smell."

"She's dead, Amelie."

"She should be brought up, buried properly in the cemetery."

"So you can appease something in yourself? Because it's not going to make any difference to the abbess."

Amelie looked uneasy.

He gave a dry laugh, trying to shake the arousal in him, the way heat was pooling in his groin despite the chilling atmosphere. "I didn't take you for one who believed in this spirit-and-ghost stuff."

"I don't. I… It's just that there's something tangible down here. I can feel…emotions." Her words were suddenly clipped—he'd irked her.

"Maybe the abbess would stop haunting the abbey and screaming up in the turrets if she was laid to rest properly," she said.

"It's wind in the turrets, Amelie. There is no ghost."

She turned her head sharply away, her mouth flat.

"Come." He took her elbow again, to guide her back to the stairs. But she resisted, stopping him.

"Tahar."

"What?"

She looked up at him, those eyes huge dark pools, her lips so close.

"I wish you would consider it one day—taking her up."

"Amelie," he said softly, "there might be bones behind that wall, then again, there might not. Maybe it's just a story, island lore. The expense of structurally stabilizing the roof down here, taking out that wall—it's not worth it."

"I don't know how you can live on top of her remains like this. Her spirit is trapped down here, and she can't move over to the other side, or whatever it is that ghosts do. It's about closure, Tahar," she whispered. "We all need closure to move on. To be at peace."

Her face was so close he could almost taste the warmth of her breath on his lips.

Suddenly he wanted to trust her—to believe she was exactly who she said she was. There was something genuine, even innocent in her. And it aroused a raw protective instinct him. He welcomed the return of these old sensations. It fuelled a new power growing in him. It gave him a sense of value. And God knew, it was a relief to feel something other than rage, however briefly.

But as he was about to speak, a scurrying sounded in the blackness. He swung his flashlight.

Amelie bumped against him again, peering into the darkness. "What was that?" she whispered.

The noise came again, nails scampering over stone.

Her hand closed around his arm. He could feel both her breasts against his torso now.

"Probably rats," he said, voice thick, husky.

"God, this place is getting to me. I'm sorry." She tried to step back, release him, but Tariq held on. Her face changed.

Almost of its own volition, his right hand reached up, touched her curls—her hair *was* soft, like silk. "It's okay," he whispered, drinking in her scent, feeling strands against his face.

She raised her face to him, her breathing becoming

light. Lust swirled darkly in Tariq and he fought the urge to go further, to press his mouth to hers, to take her upstairs, to his room.

He reminded himself she could be an imposter—he had yet to hear from Omair. And he didn't want to feel these things, to sleep with someone who could be a lie. Who had come to hurt him or his family.

Then again, maybe blind sex was what he wanted. Without the commitment. Without having to betray Julie's memory.

"Tell me what happened to your past relationship, Amelie," he whispered, needing to know more, who she really was, everything about her. "Why did you feel you needed to get away after your breakup?"

She was silent for a beat. "I'd prefer to talk upstairs, Tahar, it's creepy down here."

"Just tell me this, before we go up."

It was easier for him to ask it down here, in the dark. It felt honest—her guard was down. She was vulnerable right now. And he felt he could say things down here that he couldn't in the daylight.

"I go for the wrong men, Tahar. I thought this time was different." She took a deep breath. "We'd talked marriage. Commitment. And all the while he was screwing someone else, someone in a position to advance his career. I—" Emotion gleamed sharp and sudden in her eyes. She gave a dry laugh, raising her hand to brush away a tear that escaped. "Guess I'm more messed up by it than I thought."

He caught her hand, and wiped away the tear himself. As he touched her face, she leaned slightly into him. Tariq allowed his hand to linger, an incredible feeling surging through his body, his world clarifying in such a sharp and sudden way it startled him.

It was like finally seeing through fog. Down here, in the dark, everything seemed transparent.

"Why do you think you go for the wrong men, Amelie?" he said, softly, lowering his hand to her neck, feeling the flutter of her pulse at her carotid.

She inhaled, glanced toward the stairs. He could sense she felt trapped, but by more than just the darkness. She was locked into a pattern of behavior that was making her unhappy, and she was uncertain about whether to give in to his touch, go further.

"I don't know, Tahar," she said quietly. "I'm attracted to something physical in a man at first. Which isn't unusual, I suppose." She gave a nervous laugh. "And then the relationship becomes very physical, really fast. But when I look beyond the physicality, there's nothing more. Nothing to sustain it. Sometimes I think I like to focus on the physical to avoid looking deeper." She snorted softly. "And then the guy leaves, or it ends. And I, stupidly, feel used. Then I rinse, repeat. How pathetic is that? Except this last time I thought was different. It was exactly the same."

"You're sabotaging yourself, Amelie."

She stilled, silent for several beats. "You're saying I get what I ask for."

"I'm saying you have choices. You're making them for a reason."

She didn't reply.

"Maybe you don't want the relationships to last," he said. "Maybe you fear commitment for some underlying reason, or perhaps you don't feel worthy of a good relationship?"

She turned abruptly away from him, aiming her flashlight toward the stairs. "I need to get out of here," she said, groping her way along the wall.

Tariq watched her for a moment. He'd upset her with that last comment. He suspected it cut too close to the truth. For some reason, Amelie lacked a sense of self-worth, and he wondered why. What could this beautiful, vibrant, intelligent, compassionate young woman be wanting? What need was she seeking to fulfill in herself by her poor choices?

"You're a fine one to talk about sabotage," she called over her shoulder as she reached the steps. "You're just wallowing in your own hurt, and I think you like it that way."

Tariq followed her up the stairs. He chose not to dignify her comment with a response. She was right. But that was changing. *She* was making it change.

Outside the mist was now pouring like heavy smoke over the top of the perimeter wall that faced the sea, and the light was dim. As they walked slowly down to the old cemetery, a few dead leaves, still attached to the bare branches of trees, clicked in the mounting wind.

Bella rubbed her arms, wishing she'd brought her jacket out here. She glanced at Tariq's close protection detail moving in shadows near the wall. This was the life of royalty, she imagined, always having someone near, watching, never truly being left alone. Especially for a prince and kingdom under terrorist threat.

Perhaps that's why he craved solitude so intensely now.

"You're cold," he said. "And I've upset you."

She wrapped her arms over her stomach. "Yeah," she said. "But maybe you're right. The truth hurts."

Bella noted the way he glanced briefly at her breasts. Her nipples were tight with cold under her snug sweater, and his interest just tightened them further. There was still desire in the pitch blackness of his eye, and she'd felt a tenderness in him when he'd wiped away her tear. Despite his aloofness and anger, the healer still lurked in Tariq, as did the fires of passion. And in that moment, the realization hit her hard—she really was in some kind of love with the sheik. She, the little orphan from Chicago, was infatuated with an oil-rich and damaged prince. It was a life so far out of her league she could barely imagine living it. And it scared her, because she could see he wanted to take his desire further. So did she.

But she was also a lie.

The urge to come clean with him began to grow overpowering in Bella as she regarded his features, the mist closing in behind him like a shroud. Then she thought of the photograph in her back pocket, of what he'd do when he found out she'd taken it from his wallet.

She was still so unsure of him, and his reasons for secrecy. Or how he was linked to the senator.

"And after what I said to you, I guess I deserved it." Bella turned and went to a toppled gravestone. Crouching down, she edged the creepers aside and dusted sand off the lichen-covered stone. It was damp and cold with mist. Angling her head she tried to read the inscription carved below angel wings. It was in Latin.

He translated from over her shoulder. "It says, 'Here lies the body of Katherine Marie Dupres, 1789–1817.'"

The rest of the inscription was obscured by the blooms of rust-colored lichen.

"She was just my age when she died," Bella said, looking up, taking in the tumbled headstones around her, some choked by tangled weeds, dry brambles. A few dead leaves scuttled suddenly over grass and stone as the wind gusted more sharply and a fine rain started to fall. Bella glanced up at the bare fingers of the trees stabbing into the darkening sky above the chapel, the crucifix silhouetted on top.

Getting up, she began to walk slowly, gravestone to gravestone, the sense of past heavy, the weight of mortality sobering, the rain suddenly irrelevant. Tariq watched her in silence. He was giving her some distance. She wondered if he was thinking of Julie, buried in the States.

She dropped to her haunches again, moved a creeper back off another headstone.

"Also a Dupres," she said. "This one died earlier, in the 1700s."

"There's a whole family of Dupres buried here." He was quiet for a moment. Then he said, suddenly, "How long are you planning to take researching and writing this novel?"

"I don't know." She stood, dusting off her jeans. "As long as it takes, I guess. I have no rush to get back home—there's nothing there for me right now."

"What about family?" He glanced at the Dupres family headstone as he spoke. "Do you not have family back home?"

Bella hesitated, taken by surprise.

"I…I have family."

"You wanted to get away from them, too?"

She gave a wry smile. "I suppose I deserve that." She paused. "I don't see them as often as I should."

"Why not?"

She thought of her adoptive family—Italian-American mother and father, her brothers. They all lived in Chicago. They all met for big dinners, special occasions, birthdays, christenings, funerals. She was the one who'd left home, tried to make it somewhere else, who found excuses not to return home.

"They're scattered around the place," she lied.

"Your parents are no longer together?"

"No, they are—my mom and dad have been married almost fifty years."

"Half a century," he said, black eye regarding her intently.

Caution whispered through Bella.

Don't give too much away—not yet.

"They still love each other. Very much."

"So it's your siblings who are scattered around the place?"

His questions, his sudden personal curiosity, was making her edgy. Did he want to know because he was interested in her, or because he still wasn't certain he could trust her? Or a bit of both? Bella's thoughts went to the phone call he'd taken in his study, the look on his face when he'd exited his office and discovered her in the library. His men leaving after they'd dropped her off this morning. He *had* to be checking into her background, and the clock was ticking.

In more ways than one.

She inhaled, calculating her best course of action, fighting an overriding desire to tell him about her family in Chicago, her background. It was a strange thing, this need to share.

He took a step forward. Swaths of mist blew thicker, like gauze curtains subtly darkening the sky.

"I understand from my men that your great-grandmother's family came from this region. Is that where the name Amelie comes from? Chenard?"

Her heart beat faster. That's what she'd told Madame—it must have gotten around the village, along with the story that she was a novelist.

"No," she said.

His brow arched.

She swallowed, glancing at the gravestone near her feet, avoiding his scrutiny. "It's not technically true that my grandmother comes from here. The truth is, I have no idea if there's even French blood in my veins. I'm adopted, Tahar. I have zero idea who my real parents are, or if they're even alive."

She looked up at him, direct.

"I was two days old when I was abandoned in a bassinet in a private alcove as part of an inner-city hospital's Angel's Cradle program. It's designed as a way for young mothers, teens, to anonymously dump their newborns instead of leaving them to die somewhere. The cops are on board with the program—no questions are asked. For some reason, maybe because of some medical problems, no one wanted to adopt me, and for two years I remained in the foster system. My parents took me in when I was almost three. I think they felt sorry for me." She hesitated, hating the bitterness that had crept into her voice. She thought she was over this. But she wasn't. She'd never be. It had left a quiet hole in her psyche, a question she might never answer—who was she, where did she come from, how did she fit in?

Her need to find answers had stirred an interest in journalism. It had shaped her career. It was who she was— Bella DiCaprio, forged by an incipient longing to expose the truth. Never fully able to commit to relationships out of some buried fear she'd be abandoned again. So she destroyed those relationships first, before they could hurt her. That, she realized suddenly, was why Derek's betrayal had hit so hard. She'd finally decided to try. And she'd been abandoned anyway. By both him and the newspaper.

"My parents did love me," she said quietly. "They still do. But I've always been the outsider. Even in my own home."

"Why?"

She gave a shrug. "They already had five biological sons when they took me in. I was the only adopted one, the only girl." Guilt stabbed more sharply. They'd tried so hard to make her feel part of their family. Minnie, her adoptive mother, had named her Bella. "Because you are beautiful," she'd said.

Bella felt anything but beautiful.

"I understand," he said quietly. "Family—those blood ties—it's important. It's everything."

"Yet you've cut your own family out from your life," she said. "Or have you?"

Something flickered through his features. The misty rain was coming down a little heavier now, and it was beginning to dampen their clothes, wind gusting harder as the dead leaves finally tore loose from the bare branches. A foghorn sounded out at sea.

"My family remains key in my life." He inhaled deeply, as if considering something. Then he said, "You reminded me of that, Amelie—what you said in the library, and by the pool. I hated to hear the truth in your words. But you were right. I need to change this."

She felt awkward. She'd told him the veiled truth about her family. And she knew that he was now telling her the general truth about his. The barriers between them were thinning. Her mind went back to that family photo in her pocket, the blind king, his wife…perspiration suddenly broke out over her body.

She knew where she'd seen the queen's face before!

She had to get back to her room, her computer, to check, to be sure. She had to contact Hurley right away. This was not possible…*was it?* And if so, what on earth did it mean?

Adrenaline thrummed through her.

She stared at him, incredulous, and her pulse raced even faster. "I…I need to get going," she said abruptly. "I promised Madame I'd have Kiki back by, ah—" she checked her watch "—two o'clock. I don't want to be late."

Tariq frowned. "Amelie—"

But already she'd begun to move quickly over the grass, making for the walkway.

"Amelie!" he commanded. "Stop—wait."

She reached the walkway and his bodyguards surged

from the shadows, barring her progress. Amelie spun round to face him.

He caught up to her, took her arm.

"What's going on?"

"Nothing. I...I just lost track of the time."

It wasn't nothing. She looked spooked, pale. Her pulse was racing under his fingertips.

Had he pushed her too hard on family? Was what she told him even the truth? He believed it was—he'd seen such an open honesty in her face, a rawness in her eyes. It either had to be the truth, or she was a consummate—and very dangerous—liar.

"Fine," he said quietly, firmly. "I will show you the way to the kitchen where you can collect Kiki, then my men will take you home." He shot a quick glance at one of his bodyguards as he spoke. The man nodded, stepped out of earshot and called his other men on the radio.

Then he gave Tariq a subtle thumbs-up, which meant the men had returned with the limo, and were clear of Amelie's quarters where he'd sent them to look into her computer, and for anything else that might send up red flags.

There was a moment of panic when the chef realized Kiki was missing from the kitchen, but they found her near the garage and workshops that were once used as stables.

Tariq saw Bella to the limousine, Kiki tucked tightly into her arms. Almost losing the dog seemed to have added to her sudden nervousness. She climbed into the vehicle, distracted. He motioned for his driver to wind down her window.

Tariq leaned into the car, close. She opened her lips in surprise.

"Come for dinner tomorrow night," he said quietly.

Disquiet filled her purple eyes.

"Please," he said, even more quietly.

She moistened those lips. "On one condition," she said softly, her attention back, wholly, on him.

"And what is that condition?"

"You let me cook."

Surprise rippled through Tariq, and he felt a slow smile curve along his lips. Her attention went to his mouth, and heat pooled low in his gut.

"You like to cook?" he said.

"I saw your kitchen. Anyone would like to cook in a kitchen like that."

He studied her, as if from a fresh perspective. "You continue to surprise me, Amelie."

"I hope not, too much." Her cheeks warmed under his scrutiny and she swallowed.

"Where did you learn to cook?"

"My mother. I spent my childhood among the steaming pots in the kitchen. It was always the heart of our home, but there was never a recipe in sight. She taught me to use the senses—taste, smell. The herbs have to feel just right in your fingers."

"All right," he said, still watching her closely. "But I have a condition of my own."

"No dog?"

He laughed. "No, I don't mind the dog at all—I told you, I like animals. My condition is that you tell my driver what ingredients you need before he drops you off. He'll pass the list on to my chef. Whatever you require will be waiting when you arrive tomorrow."

She opened her mouth, but he stepped back, making a quick sign for the driver to close the window. The glass hummed quietly up and the limo began to draw away.

Bella turned in her seat to watch him as they exited the grim iron gates. He stood at the abbey entrance, like the sheik he was, proud, tall, dark, the spires reaching into the gray mist above him. Somehow, thought Bella, at that moment, Tariq Al Arif looked just a little less broken.

And she'd fallen even more deeply for him. If that was possible.

She cursed softly, closed her eyes. What a pathetic, stupid, ridiculous infatuation. A prince? A kingdom? She—little orphan Bella from Chicago—couldn't even *begin* to think of herself in that context. Blogger Bella with no real job. Bella, with university degrees worth nothing and debts out the yin yang. Bella, who was going to wreck his life and his family's with her scoop, because if the woman in the photo really was who she thought it might be, it was going to rock both his kingdom, and her country.

It had the power to depose the man set to be the next president of the United States.

Chapter 7

The first thing Bella did upon returning to her room was open her laptop.

It had been accessed. She could tell by checking the properties of the files in there, what time they'd last been opened.

Tariq's men had been here, in her room. They'd poked around in her computer, touched her things.

She lurched to her feet, wrapping her arms tight across her stomach. Then she swiveled, dropped to her knees, pried up the floorboard. Her passport, driver's license, credit card, wad of cash, were just as she'd left them.

But had they *seen* her ID? Was Tariq, at this very moment, being told of her real identity?

From the back pocket of her jeans Bella removed the photograph she'd stolen from his wallet and set it on her desk. She took the flash drive off the chain around her neck and slotted it into her laptop. Scrolling quickly through the flash-drive files, she searched for the digital scan of the newspaper article and photograph taken at a medical convention in Chicago more than ten years ago.

Bella clicked on the file. The image opened, filled her screen. She enlarged the photo and reached for the family shot she'd taken from Tariq's wallet. Comparing the two side by side Bella's hands began to shake. Quickly she opened her Skype program and clicked on Hurley's video-call icon.

No answer.

Bella checked her watch. D.C. was six hours behind— Hurley should be awake and in the office. Digitally, she cropped the image part of the article, saved it as a separate file and tried Hurley again.

Still no answer.

Tension twisted through her. She grabbed her cell, punched in the emergency number Hurley had sent her for his own prepaid phone. He picked up on the fourth ring.

"Hurley, thank God."

"Bella?" A pause. "You okay?"

"Are you near your laptop?"

"It's in the other room—I'm using it only to connect with you. Hang up and I'll video call you right back. I don't want to stay on this phone too long—I don't know how far they'll go to trace you." He hesitated. "There's been a strange van in the street outside for a couple of days. I'm worried they're tapping into the phones."

While she waited, Bella connected her small portable scanner to her laptop. Inserting Tariq's family photo, she pressed Scan. The image began to roll through. She saved the file to a folder on the flash drive.

An electronic sound announced Hurley's call. She hit Accept, and as his round face filled the small screen she felt a punch of warmth, solidarity. Hurley, Scoob, Agnes—the Watchdog crew had become a family to her.

"I'm sending you another image, Hurley. It's a face I've cropped from a group family photo. It's small, but I'm hoping you can still run it through your facial-recognition software and compare it to other known images." She loaded the file to Skype as she spoke, hit Send. "I need to be sure it's who I think it is."

She *was* sure—she just couldn't wrap her head around it.

"Who's the cropped photo supposed to be of?" Hurley asked as he waited for the file to download on his end.

"The queen of Al Na'Jar," she said quietly. "Without a veil."

"You're kidding—no one's ever seen her face."

"Well, it's in *this* photo. A candid shot of the royal family. I sort of borrowed it from Tariq's wallet." Bella uploaded a second file as she spoke. "This next photo I'm sending is the one I want you to compare her to."

"Okay, I've opening them both fi— Jesus!" His brow furrowed as he studied the images. "Queen Nikki Al Arif is *Alexis Etherington?*"

"Senator Sam Etherington's missing ex-wife."

He stared at her.

Bella leaned forward. "I don't know what this means, Hurley, but the senator divorced her and had her declared dead in absentia before marrying and fathering children with his current wife. Meanwhile, Alexis could be alive, living under an alias and married to King Zakir, who controls the very same country Sam Etherington is expecting an oil deal with. And," she said quietly, "there's the allegation that Etherington might also have been involved in an attempted assassination of King Zakir's brother, Omair.

At least, this was where Althea Winston was leading us before she was killed."

Hurley drew his hand over his mouth, the movement pulling his lips down into a frown as he stared at the images.

"Can you run that face through the biometrics software—is it detailed enough?"

He nodded. "We'll pull up some other old images of Dr. Alexis Etherington as well, and compare those. I mean, she *could* just be a startling look-alike."

"I know, but the coincidences of the queen being a dead ringer for a woman standing next to Tariq at a medical conference ten years ago—an ophthalmic surgeon who just happens to be a specialist in the genetic blindness that afflicts the royal family?"

Hurley whistled softly, shaking his head.

"Alexis Etherington vanished off the face of this earth a year after she claimed she was run off a bridge by a black SUV with no plates, just like Althea Winston was. And King Zakir's new wife—a mysterious Norwegian—shows up out of the blue years later, and never reveals her face."

"The queen does have a background—"

"Like Amelie has a background? Maybe someone faked an ID, a past history for her."

"You think the Al Arifs know who she actually is—I mean, *if* it's the same woman?"

"Hell knows what's going on, Hurley. But if it's true, this alone could derail the senator's bid for the White House."

"I'll call you as soon as I've run these through our system." Hurley paused. "What if Senator Etherington and his ex are in on this together—maybe that's why he's promising oil from Al Na'Jar and new alliances in the Middle East?"

She swore softly, dragging her hand through her hair

as she thought. "I don't know. Something weird is going on here." She breathed in deep. "I need to talk to him."

"Tariq?"

She bit her lip, nodded. "He's suspicious of me. He kept me busy with a tour of the abbey while his men poked around my room and computer—thank God it was clean. But I don't know if they found my passport and ID, and I figure he's running a deeper background check on Amelie as we speak. If he's not on to me yet, he will be soon. I need to keep the lines of dialogue open—but the more I deceive him, the less likely he'll be to trust me, or talk to me down the road. I think I might need to come clean with him now."

"Bella—" Hurley's voice was grave. "Telling Tariq who you are could be dangerous. Something huge is going on with his family, and Etherington, and the U.S. election. And STRIKE. Just look at that JFK bombing. Look at what happened to Althea Winston after she contacted you, and to her husband. Tariq's family might go to extremes to stop you if they know who you are, and what you want." He paused. "You were already attacked once, by men who spoke Arabic and carried a traditional dagger when—"

"That couldn't have been his family," she interrupted. "He'd know who I was then, surely?"

"Not necessarily, not by sight."

She thought of his bodyguards, the deadpan faces, the impenetrable black eyes. The weapons they carried. Nausea curled in her stomach.

"Bella, he could kill you."

"I don't think he would, Hurley. I feel he—"

I feel that he cares for me. He's attracted to me, and I don't want to blow it all. But how stupid am I to think I could even have a chance with him...

"Maybe not him, but others connected with him. This

is a powerful family, Bella. They protect each other, and that might include doing whatever it takes to protect the queen's secret."

Family—those blood ties—it's everything, Amelie.

"You should get out of there now, while you can—just run with what we've got, especially if the queen's biometrics match Alexis Etherington's."

"No," she said quietly. "I need his side of the story. I'm a journalist, that's my job if I'm doing it properly. And I owe it to him if he's clean in all this."

Hurley's mouth flattened. He stared at her in silence for several beats. "What you're doing could scuttle the U.S. presidential election, Bella. People have already died."

"I know," she whispered.

"Please, be careful."

She nodded.

"Wipe your Skype files. Keep everything on that flash drive. You have access to a safe?"

"Estelle Dubois has a fire safe. I'll ask her if I can store my drive in there. She doesn't have a computer, knows nothing about them, so there's no chance she'll try and look into it. I'll tell her it contains a draft of my novel."

"Tariq doesn't know you took his family photo?"

"Not yet," she said, very quietly.

Then, as she was about to kill the call, he said, "Bella—" Something in his voice changed.

"Look, I know how badly you want to go mainstream, how badly you want a paying job. This will take you *and* the website mainstream. It *will* start to pay."

"Hurley, I'm committed to breaking this on my blog."

"Promise."

"I promise," she said.

Bella signed off, rubbed her brow. It seemed ridiculous to break a story of this magnitude on an obscure conspiracy-theorist website. But she had to. She had to find a way to leverage it. She couldn't betray Hurley and the crew. Not now. Yet it went against every journalistic instinct. It went against her key goals, the reason she'd come here. But she wouldn't even be here without Hurley, Scoob, Agnes.

She heaved out a sigh, cleaned up her Skype history again, opened up a fresh Word file on the flash drive. She began to write down notes, thinking how best to approach Tariq with the truth. But all she could see in her mind was an image of Tariq standing in front of the abbey gates as she'd been driven out the gates this afternoon. She touched her cheek where he'd wiped away a tear. Emotion rode hard in her chest.

When she revealed who she was, at bare minimum he was going to cut her out.

Family is key.

This is a powerful family, Bella...

She inhaled deeply. Tomorrow night, when she went for dinner—that's when she had to do it.

Removing the flash drive she curled her fist around it and sat there for a while, weighing her options. Then she lurched to her feet and began pacing her small quarters.

She essentially had two big stories she could run with if Tariq—or the palace—chose not to comment. One was that the MagMo assassination attempt on Sheik Tariq Al Arif had failed to kill him, and the heir to the oil-rich kingdom of Al Na'Jar was alive, scarred and hiding in France. That the palace had lied. She had the photos and biometrics to prove it was him.

The other story—if Hurley's facial-recognition software confirmed it—was that Senator Sam Etherington's ex-wife was not dead, either, and was now married to the blind king of a country under MagMo attack, the same country

Etherington was promising a lucrative oil deal with. If she could only find a way to speak to the queen—she might finally find out what had happened, and who had tried to run Alexis off that bridge, and why.

Bella chewed on her lip. And how did this link to STRIKE and the senator's apparent involvement in an assassination attempt on the youngest brother, Omair Al Arif?

Just who was in bed with who?

Nerves twitched through her stomach. Tariq was going to hate her.

Bella stopped pacing. What made it worse was she *wanted* him to like her.

And tomorrow night her revelation was going to end the small, tremulous but very real connection that had been growing between them.

She gave a snort. *Yeah, Bella, a connection between Amelie and Tahar—neither of them are real. It's fiction. All lies. You're a nothing orphan from Chicago, and you're dreaming of a prince?*

Get real.

She had to stick to her core reasons for coming here. Get the story—go big, make a name, get a real job, earn a living. Take care of herself.

Because no one else was going to do it for her.

Tightening her mouth, she firmed her resolve. Then she went to the main house to ask Estelle Dubois if she could lock her USB drive in the safe.

Isaiah Gold studied the digital image his surveillance team had just forwarded to his laptop—a photo of queen Nikki Al Arif without a veil.

The file had been entered into the Watchdog facial-recognition program, and it had come up as a match against several older photographs of Dr. Alexis Etherington. He rubbed his jaw, thinking. Not only had Bella DiCaprio found Tariq Al Arif alive, she now knew what The Moor knew—that the queen of Al Na'Jar was Sam Etherington's ex.

Did she also know Sam had tried to have his ex killed? That he'd inadvertently murdered his own twins in the process?

Up until this point, this knowledge had been Aban Ghaffar's trump card, his blackmail tool. Ghaffar's way of securing Sam's cooperation both now, and into the future. It was Ghaffar's way of ensuring the future president's commitment to militarily back a coup that would overthrow Al Na'Jar, and put the kingdom and all its oil in his control.

In return, during the proposed coup, Ghaffar's promise was to have the queen eliminated along with the rest of the remaining royal family. Sam would then finally be free of the specter of his ex. Because as long as she remained out there, she would always be a Sword of Damocles hanging over the future president's head. There would always be the potential for blackmail, a chance Sam could still go down for murder, and conspiracy to commit murder.

But if DiCaprio ran this story about Alexis and Sam now, she would effectively cut the balls off Ghaffar, leave him with zero control over Sam. The Moor would lose U.S. backing to take control of Al Na'Jar, yet Sam would still go down. And Isaiah himself would lose his prospects as a behind-the-scenes presidential advisor, the quiet ruling hand in the Oval Office. The puppet master.

It was in *all* their interests to stop Bella DiCaprio before she could run with this story. Already it was spiraling out of their control—she'd shared this photo with the Watchdog crew. Several people now knew Sam's secret. That meant too many loose ends.

Isaiah ran his tongue over his teeth. DiCaprio had not sent this image via any of the computers connected to the Watchdog server. It had been introduced to the system via an external storage device, then run through the biometrics software. She was being careful. But not careful enough.

He picked up his encrypted phone, called New York.

"Are you near your computer? You need to see this." He clicked Send.

A few moments of silence hung between the lines as the image was downloaded into a computer in Ghaffar's plush Manhattan penthouse. A powerhouse.

"Where did this come from?" Ghaffar asked.

"DiCaprio. She knows about Alexis Etherington."

Silence.

Isaiah swallowed, loosened his tie. Few people in this world made him uneasy—Aban Ghaffar was one.

"Does the senator know about this?"

"Not yet."

"Can you keep it that way?"

Isaiah knew what Ghaffar was getting at—if Sam found out a reporter had the information, it stole The Moor's power over him.

"If we nip this in the bud," Isaiah said, "before it can become an issue, then there is no need for the senator to know. I'd rather not have him distracted from his campaign at this stage."

This statement put Isaiah in a slightly elevated position over both Sam and Ghaffar. He liked it this way. Another beat of silence.

"Any leads as to where she is yet?"

"She called a prepaid cell in the Watchdog building. My surveillance team outside the building picked it up with surveillance equipment, and traced the area code to France. But she signed off before they could triangulate further."

"France," Ghaffar said quietly. "And you say this was from your CIA surveillance guys?"

Isaiah moistened his lips. "Black ops, culled from CIA and STRIKE intelligence, on a need-to-know basis only. They believe they're on a terrorist surveillance mission, and they're answerable to a middle man—no overt link to me or Sam. Or you."

Aban stared at the photo of the queen, thinking Isaiah was going to be an invaluable tool in the White House, and a way for him to influence the most powerful office in the world—as long as he kept hold over this information.

"I thought it was France," he said softly as he continued to stare at the photo. "I already have men on standby in Paris. We have meteorological information that matches the conditions along the Brittany coast at the precise time the photo of Tariq was taken." He paused. "We're narrowing it down. My men will take care of Tariq and DiCaprio as soon as we find them. We'll need to eliminate the Watchdog team as well."

"If we take the Watchdog crew out too soon, we lose our link to DiCaprio."

"Then we use them as leverage first."

He heard Isaiah inhale, and Aban smiled. "Don't worry," he said quietly. "The men we used in the attempt to take DiCaprio—I will use them again. You can keep your hands clean that way. But your surveillance team will need to stand down when we're ready to move in on the crew."

Silence.

"Mr. Gold," Aban said coolly. "Fear not, my men are dispensable. Their cells stateside are tightly compartmentalized. They do not know my identity. If the proverbial scat hits the fan, law enforcement will find only MagMo fundamentalists." He paused. "But should *you* expose me… well, I keep careful records."

"Likewise."

Ghaffar smiled. "We make a good team, then."

Tariq positioned his lower back against the padded seat of the chest press in his gym, feet planted firmly apart. The room was bright, mirrors bouncing light back at him. He wore only his black gym shorts, a white towel around his neck, his body supple from a swim. Outside the floor-to-ceiling windows that looked out over the sea, silvery streams of rain snaked down the panes.

He reached for the handles at chest level, his right hand finding an easy grip. Tariq angled his crippled fingers around the other handle, breathed in deep. Slowly he pressed outward, trying not to let his right side dominate his left, struggling to make the injured half of his body work in tandem with his good side.

Muscles stretched against scarred tissue, against disuse, but slowly he found a rhythm borne of intense focus. Sweat poured off him as he pumped the weights, harder, faster, his chest burning. He caught his reflection, his dark skin shining, his black hair wet—no eye patch. A ferocity filled him and he used it to push harder. He was doing too much, too soon, he knew that. But he couldn't stop. All he could see when he closed his eye, when he felt the burn, was Amelie.

He could imagine the taste of her mouth, smell her shampoo, the feel of her body under his. He pumped harder, blood roaring in his ears as he struggled to burn off the attraction.

Finally he let the weights drop with a clang and he slumped against the seat, sweat dripping. He *couldn't* chase her from his thoughts. He could not beat out the desire building in him. It was just physical, he told himself—it did nothing to diminish the memory of Julie.

Irritably he reached for the television remote, clicked a button. A large satellite TV screen mounted in the far corner of his gym flickered to life. He found the CNN channel. Tariq had been out of touch with the world since the bomb blast ten months ago, and he felt a need to reconnect. Subliminally he blamed this, too, on Amelie.

He got to his feet, toweling off, thinking that not only was he trying to chest-press her out of his mind, he wanted to get fit, look good for her. Tariq swore softly in Arabic, then glanced up sharply as the CNN newscast segued into coverage of the U.S. presidential campaign, cutting to footage of Senator Sam Etherington alighting from his campaign bus.

Distaste filled Tariq's mouth.

The broadcast cut to a clip of Etherington talking about homeland security, and then about energy and oil. How he would bring new allies from the Middle East to the table, and how there was potential for an agreement with the newly oil-rich kingdom of Al Na'Jar. Tariq stilled, towel in hand, and he frowned. The guy was in for a rude awakening—Al Na'Jar was *not* his friend.

So what made him think he could talk like this?

Tariq flicked through several more channels—all covering the election, all talking about Sam Etherington as if the sociopathic narcissist was already the president. He stopped as he hit another newscast. A blonde anchorwoman was saying, "There are still no leads in the accident that claimed the life of Althea Winston and her five-year-old daughter, Della Johnson. Winston's tragic death comes mere months after her husband, Travis Johnson, was shot execution-style in an underground parking lot. There have been no leads in his murder, either."

A chill slaked through his chest.

Travis Johnson had been Faith's STRIKE handler. He'd

been shot by men on a motorbike as Omair had been trying to question him about who'd ordered the hits on him and Faith. But Johnson had died with the secret on his lips. And now his wife was dead?

Tariq reached for his T-shirt, yanking it over his head as he went rapidly to his office. He punched in Omair's number.

"Did you hear the news?" he said the instant his brother picked up. "Althea Winston, Travis Johnson's widow—she's dead. Run off a bridge with her daughter in the car."

Omair was silent for a moment. "You're sure?"

"It's all over the news."

"She must have known something," Omair said softly. "Johnson could have let something slip, some pillow talk. I should have gone back, pressed her."

Tariq raked his hand over his damp hair. "No, Omair. She had her child with her—you did the right thing. Her death *could* have been an accident."

"Or she might have tried to talk to someone, let slip that she had incriminating information. She could have told me who ordered my assassination—whether it came from high up, or a rogue faction within STRIKE." Omair cursed softly. Then he said, "So you were watching the news?"

Tariq inhaled slowly. He knew what his brother was getting at—it was becoming clear that Tariq was reengaging in life, in politics, reconnecting with a sense of royal duty. But he changed the subject, preferring not to discuss it. "Anything yet on Amelie Chenard?"

"My P.I. is due to call me with his results day after tomorrow. I'll let you know as soon as I have word. Just keep her close meantime. Was there anything on her computer?"

"Research files on the history of the abbey, the murder of the abbess, some notes on Ile-en-Mer."

"No email history? Contact list? No parts of her novel—nothing else?"

"No."

Omair hesitated. "That's unusual, Tariq. Be careful."

"I will."

But as Tariq hung up, he knew—innocent or not—on some level he was already sunk with Amelie.

And he *needed* her to be innocent because of it.

Wanting to get a head start on a marinade for the lamb she planned to cook, Bella arrived at the abbey early. Nerves bit at her as she rang the bell at the abbey gate.

If Tariq had been clued in to her true identity by now, she could be walking into a trap. And if he didn't know, she might be creating a trap of her own by returning his family photo and confessing her real reason for being here.

Before she left Madame's place, Hurley had called to confirm the facial-recognition match between Alexis Etherington and Queen Nikki Al Arif. This information was burning in Bella's chest now, along with her nerves.

Scoob had also discovered that fifteen years ago Benjamin Raber had been CEO of Armstech, a manufacturer of military-grade weapons and security installations. At the same time, Etherington had been on the Armstech board, working as a lawyer for the corporation. It was during this period that a sexual assault charge was brought against Raber.

According to Hurley, it was not the first time Raber had gotten rough with prostitutes, and it looked like the charge was going to stick. But Etherington appeared to have made the charges miraculously go away. The prostitute in question had then drowned in an "accident" later the same year.

"This could mean that Sam Etherington has power over Raber," Hurley had told Bella earlier on Skype. "And Travis Johnson apparently took his orders from Raber. At the very least, we now know there's an intimate connection between the STRIKE boss, and the probable next U.S. president."

The gates swung slowly open and Bella wheeled her bike down the gravel driveway through the rain.

Scoob had also learned that Raber was being touted in some circles as Etherington's pick for Ambassador-at-Large for Counterterrorism.

This new information fed into Bella's anxiety as the butler let her into the abbey. It could mean that Sam Etherington himself had ordered Omair Al Arif's assassination—if Althea Winston had been telling the truth.

"Monsieur Tahar is not expecting you yet—he's in the gym," the butler said as he showed Bella in. She caught a look in the butler's eyes, a slight smile on his lips. There was something accessible about the man today, something had softened in him toward her.

He led her to the kitchen, where the chef was also in an upbeat and friendly mood today. Bella had met him yesterday when she'd come looking for Kiki and his demeanor had been guarded, watchful. Now his smile was hearty and warm as he greeted her and showed her the table of ingredients she'd requested. There was prosciutto, eggplant, cheeses, olive oil, balsamic vinegar, tomatoes and fresh herbs among the spread, along with two bottles of the red wine she'd asked for.

"All yours," he said in French. "Aprons are over there if you need one."

"Does he have any dietary taboos?" she asked.

Chef shook his head. "*Non,* the monsieur is a connoisseur of fine food, wines—" he gave a shrug "—but he has not been interested in much. Until now."

"You knew him from before? I mean, before his accident?"

A flicker of the old guardedness reentered his eyes. "Yes, I have known him awhile."

"You like him," she said.

A moment of seriousness. "We all like him. We've all been worried about him." He turned to go, hesitated. "You want the radio off?"

It was playing soft classic rock. She grinned. "No, I'm used to noisy, friendly kitchens."

He nodded, grinned and left.

Bella tied on an apron and busied herself making marinade, crushing garlic, rubbing coarse salt and pepper into a leg of lamb, slicing and grilling eggplant, dousing it in oil and vinegar, chopping tomatoes. She found herself humming and moving to a punchy old tune as the hour ticked by. Locating a corkscrew she opened a bottle of wine so it could start breathing. She knew Tariq liked red, but this time she'd stayed away from Chateau Luneau, going instead with an Italian choice her father and eldest brother routinely endorsed with much gusto.

As she worked her adoptive mother's voice sifted in her consciousness. "You take this much oregano, like so, Bella." As she spoke, her mother would pinch the freshly chopped green herbs between her fingers, showing Bella, the scent fragrant in the kitchen. "And a handful of basil, like this." The basil grew in pots along the windowsill, along with tiny bright chili plants. "And just a splash of balsamic, like so. Here, taste it now—" she'd say, holding out a wooden spoon rich and red with sauce.

Bella's eyes burned suddenly, the warm memories blindsiding her. That longing, that quiet hole in her psyche, that need to know where she came from was still there in spite of the love she'd been given by Minnie DiCaprio. It was a yearning so simple, yet so complex, and it reared up its head at the most unexpected moments. Tariq had cracked something open inside her with his questions and talk of family. And it had made her vulnerable.

She felt guilt, too. Because she did, truly, love her Di-Caprio clan even though she didn't go home as often as she should.

Bella slipped the roast into the oven, put a copper pot of water to boil, set the timer and wiped her hands on a cloth. She glanced at the clock on the wall—time for a glass of wine. She reached for the open bottle and poured two glasses as she bopped her hips to a pacey late-'70s song, singing the words along with the male vocalist as she did… She reached for a glass, took a sip of wine. It was good. She untied her apron, turned around and froze.

He stood there. In the doorway, a dark, brooding shadow. Watching her.

Her heart skittered.

"How—how long have you been standing there?"

Tariq entered the kitchen, a strange intensity on his face. Bella swallowed.

"Long enough," he said, voice thick.

Her cheeks heated. She wanted to smile, say something casual, easy, but the look in his features stopped her. "Long enough for what?" she whispered, thinking of his men in her room, going through her computer. The photo in her bag. Did he know?

His gaze held hers. He come closer—very close. Bella reached behind herself, bracing against the counter where she knew there was a knife. Even so, a dark carnal ribbon of desire unfurled inside her. The kitchen felt warm. The pot was beginning to steam, the scent of the roast crisping filled the air.

"I was about to come and find you." Her voice came out hoarse. "I was going to bring you some wine."

He said nothing. Lust etched into his features, turning his eye black as oil. Bella swallowed.

He reached past her, the inside of his arm brushing her shoulder. She could smell soap, feel his heat. His hair was damp. He picked up a glass of wine, held it out to her in a toast. *"Santé,"* he whispered.

Bella inhaled, chinked her glass against his, her gaze meeting his, as they both took a deep sip. He was watching her lips. His mouth was so close. Heat arrowed to her stomach and suddenly she couldn't think straight.

"This is good," he said, glancing down at the label.

"My father's and brother's favorite." She watched his Adam's apple work as he took another swallow.

"I...I came early," she explained. "I wanted to get started on the dinner—your butler showed me in."

"I know."

What else did he know? She had to come out, say it. Now.

"Tahar, I need to—"

But he touched her mouth with his fingertips, taking the glass from her hands. "Not now," he whispered, moving his body up against hers. "Don't talk."

Bella felt the insides of her stomach begin to tremble as heat blossomed through her groin and her nipples ached. She began to throb with a need that rose from her center, and suddenly she couldn't breathe. She knew once she did talk this would be over. Maybe it was the same for him. And a lust rose so forceful it was mind-blowing—she wanted him. All of him. Inside her. She wanted to wrap herself around him, feel him move naked in her arms. She'd loved him from afar for so many months. Now he was here, his body hot, hard. Real. Against hers. But maybe only for a fleeting moment.

He cupped the back of her head, threading his fingers into her thick hair, pulling her head back. She felt his powerful thighs press against her body. His biceps were iron-hard under his black T-shirt, his skin dark against her pale sweater.

He tilted her chin up with his thumb, lowered his mouth, touched his lips to hers.

Bella's world spiraled so fast she thought she'd faint. She hooked her arms around his neck, drew him down, kissing him back, opening her mouth under his. She felt his tongue, teasing the inside seam of her lips, then he entered her mouth, deep. Her knees turned to water. She arched her back, pressing against him, holding him closer as her tongue tangled with his, and she could feel the hard, hot length of his erection against her pelvis.

Suddenly, with a strength that startled her, he lifted her onto the kitchen counter, her short skirt riding high up her hips as her bare legs opened around his thighs. She kissed him harder, more desperately. Behind her a salt-and-pepper pot knocked over, rolled off the counter, crashed to the ground. The pot on the stove started a rolling boil, steam rising through the kitchen, melding with the rich fragrances of rosemary and garlic. In the back of her mind Bella noted the heat would have to be turned down soon or the roast would burn, but desire wiped her mind clean as she felt his hand on her bare thigh. He groaned as his fingers touched skin. She wrapped her booted legs around him, emotion burning fierce in both of them, electricity crackling through their bodies as the music on the radio changed to a thrusting rock. His hand went higher up her thigh. A buzzing sounded in the distance of Bella's mind. He kissed harder. She tasted blood, didn't care. The buzzing grew louder and a burning scent fingered down into her consciousness, and with shock she realized it was the timer—the meat was burning.

Bella pulled back, breathless, lips swollen. "Oh, God." She laughed. "The roast!"

She wriggled free, hopped to the ground, opened the oven and heat billowed out. Grabbing an oven glove, she removed the roast as he turned off the buzzer and took the boiling pot off the stove.

Her heart was hammering, her cheeks flushed with the heat, a sudden awkwardness rushing through her. "It's fine—we got it in time," she said to the roast, unable to meet his eyes, fearful of the power of her own lust and rawness of emotion. Of the deception between them.

"I put it high to seal it." She covered the pan loosely with foil as she spoke. Turning the heat down, she returned the roast to the oven. "It'll be fine on low now for a while."

She set the oven glove on the counter. He came up behind her, placing his hand over hers on the glove. Bella swallowed.

"Tahar," she said quietly, struggling with the use of his alias now. "I need to tell you something. We…need to talk."

"Amelie." He took her by the shoulders, turning her gently to face him.

"Come with me," he whispered. "Let's go to the pool room."

Chapter 8

Tariq left the room in darkness but he put on the underwater lights, dimming them to a haunting glow. Outside, the sky was dark and low with clouds, rain lashing at the abbey and running in silver streams down the windows. Bella could almost hear, feel, the distant heave and push of the waves crashing and sucking at the base of the cliffs below. And beyond the soft notes of a cello concerto feeding into the pool room sound system, she could hear the eerie moan of wind in the turrets.

Tariq took her by the hand, and led her barefoot to the edge of the bubbling whirlpool. Steam rose gently from the surface of the water and the air was warm, humid.

Bella turned to him, burning with a need to confess who she was, but he placed two fingers on her lips and shook his head. "No words," he whispered, drawing her closer, sliding his hand under her sweater.

Bella's pulse began to race as he lifted her sweater slowly up over her head, his warm skin brushing against hers. Holding his gaze, Bella reached behind her back and unclasped her bra. Tariq's eye darkened to a pitch as her breasts swelled free. She dropped her bra to the floor and then unzipped her skirt, letting it fall to her bare feet. Still holding his gaze, she rolled her lace panties down her hips, and dropped them to the floor along with her skirt. His breathing became light and he stepped closer to her.

"You're beautiful," he said, placing the palm of his right hand on her hip, sliding it over her curve and round to the small of her back, then down the swell of her buttocks, drawing her hips against his. Heat pooled like fire low in her belly.

"I thought you said no words," she whispered hoarsely as she began to lift his T-shirt over his chest. She could feel the hot, hard, length of his arousal pressing firmly against her bare hips, and a wild urgency filled her, but she forced herself to move slowly, to savor every moment of being with him—this prince she'd only dared dream about. Under her hands, his skin was supple, smooth, firm. Bella dropped his black T-shirt to the floor and traced her fingers gently over the scars down the side of his torso. She felt him tense as she touched the injuries, and she thought again of that photo she'd spent so many hours staring at over the past months, falling into a deep infatuation. And now he was here, in her arms, even if for just this moment. And she wasn't going to blow it by talking. Because suddenly Bella no longer wanted to confess right now who she was—she didn't want to destroy this.

Moving her hands lower, she unzipped his pants, sliding one hand inside. She moaned as she felt him, hard, hot. Her urgency spiked, and her breathing became light, pressure building low and fierce in her abdomen. Bella quickly slid his pants down his hips. His stomach was hard and his thighs muscular, strong, his skin dusky. She moved her hand along the inside of his thighs, stroking him as she kissed the hollow at the base of his neck, teasing his skin with her tongue. He groaned suddenly and grabbed her by the back of her head, thrusting his fingers deep into her curls and jerking her hard up against his naked body. Bella could feel his heart hammering a wild staccato beat against her breasts. He tilted her head back, lowering his mouth to hers, forcing her lips open, kissing her hard, fierce, hungry, deep, as he moved her backward toward the whirlpool.

Kissing fiercely, tongues tangling, they stepped into the warm water, lowering their bodies into the tickling bubbles. The waves rippled warm and sensual over bare skin, and Bella drew back for a moment, catching her breath, her heart pumping, her lips burning, her body aching inside for him. She looked into his face, and cupped the injured side of his cheek, her heart full of compassion and desire, and she knew he could feel it in her touch, see it in her eyes. Because he inhaled deeply, closing his eye, leaning into her as she teased her fingers down the length of the scar on his cheek, slowly going lower, lower, her eyes holding his, until she reached the downward curve of his lips.

He moved his head suddenly to the side, snaring the tip of her fingers in his teeth. He bit softly, then took two fingers into his mouth, caressing her with his tongue, sucking her in deeper. Her nipples went taut, a reciprocal feeling arrowing between her legs where the water was warm, moving, and bubbles caressed. She could feel his erection pressing against her bare thigh, feel the tickle of the small gold pendant buoyant between her breasts.

In the mirrors along the one side she could see their reflection, a yin yang of male and female, alabaster skin against dusk. The notes of the cello rose in crescendo and her heart beat faster, her breathing coming lighter. Bella didn't want to think about anything beyond this moment.

She wanted to steal it, savor it, devour it before their worlds crashed down around them.

He leaned in, bringing his mouth down to hers, and this time his kiss was so gentle, so slow, it made her want to scream with need inside. He cupped her breasts, teasing her nipples, and she closed her eyes, sinking lower into the warm water as his tongue tangled with hers. His hand moved down her waist, along her hip, to her thigh, then he cupped her gently between her legs. Bella's mind spun. She opened her legs and he teased her, the combination of warm, swirling water and his fingers driving her wild. He slid a finger up into her, then another and she couldn't breathe.

"No," she whispered against his lips, about to shatter around his fingers. "I...want it to last."

She straddled him loosely instead, felt his arousal tickling, teasing her as currents of water moved between them. Bella touched his eye patch. It was wet, like his hair, which slicked back off his aristocratic, high brow.

"May I?" she whispered.

He stilled, said nothing. Gently, she took it off.

His eyelid was closed, a little depressed into the socket. She realized he had no eye at all. Emotion surged fierce into her chest.

"There," Bella whispered as she put the wet patch on the side of the pool. "Now I can see all of you." She leaned in, breasts pushing against his hard pecs. "And I want all of you." She lowered her mouth as she held his face. Pressing her lips to his, she slid her tongue into his mouth, teasing his lips as she sank slowly down onto his erection. She widened her thighs, going lower, lower, and gasped, throwing her head back with pleasure when he was fully inside her. She held still for a while, nerves tingling throughout her entire body as she adjusted the size and heat of him inside her.

Then she began rocking her pelvis against his, milking him with her muscles, the movement making the water suck and splash around them. The nerves inside Bella grew hotter as she increased friction, growing more sensitive, and she moved faster, kissing him now, fiercely, her movements turning aggressive, desperate. He bucked his hips up, meeting her thrusts, her rhythm, his shoulder muscles rolling smooth under her hands. Outside the wind rose, and rain battered in bursts against the glass.

Bella moved harder, breathless, heat pricking over her skin, throwing her head back, mouth open, the need inside her growing almost preternatural. An incredible pressure soared into her chest, into her throat. Her vision swirled into shades of scarlet and black as the cello concerto rose in crescendo, the pace of the music growing angry, deep, fast. Loud.

And abruptly, she came, digging her fingers into his skin, arching her back, head back as she cried out loud, her muscles releasing in rolling contractions that seized the length of her body.

It cracked something in him. Tariq swung her sharply round, water sloshing over the side as the cello music grew restless, edgy, and the wind began to scream in the turrets. He slipped one hand beneath the small of her back and braced against the pool wall with the other as he thrust into her, crushing her against him, as if he could beat away the things that haunted him with sheer, pounding force. His shoulder muscles felt strong after his swim, he felt powerful inside her. But she was lean, strong, and though small in his arms she met his rhythm, thrust for thrust, wrapping him up with her legs, hooking her ankles behind his back, pulling him in deeper and deeper.

It only made him more desperate and he moved almost wildly, waves rippling from them into the pool. Deep in the far recesses of his mind, Tariq knew this was wrong, that he should wait to hear from Omair, that he should not be doing this without telling her who he really was. But he was afraid Omair's news would be bad, and he wanted her, *Amelie,* like she said she was. He bucked harder, fiercer, driving his pain into dark corners, finding his strength, his raw power. She arched suddenly against him, gasping as she came again. And he could no longer control the exquisite, painful pleasure building inside him. He stilled for a moment, unable to move, quivering hot inside her, then as he watched her face, he grabbed her buttocks, yanking her tight against him as he released into her with a low groan of pleasure.

Tariq felt liberated, a strange lightness in his limbs as he gathered her into his arms. Her body was now soft, relaxed, supple, a magical luminosity to her face. And he just held her in the warm water like that, emotion pricking into his eye—sweet, poignant, exquisite.

She was watching him.

"Are you okay?" she whispered.

He smiled softly and kissed her face, moving a wet strand of hair off her brow. "More than okay," he said gently. "You make me forget. You make me feel whole."

He kissed her again, a million feelings racing through him. After seeing her in the kitchen like that, long boots to her knees, short skirt, body-hugging sweater, bopping her hips to that tune, surrounded by the warmth of the kitchen, the scents of hearth and home… He'd been unable to stop himself.

The fact that she responded to him like she had—it ignited a fire in him that would not be quelled.

He'd tried to tell himself, somewhere in the distance of

his lust-thickened brain, that it was just sex. Just physical. It was no betrayal of Julie's memory. That it didn't have to mean anything.

But it did. She really had made him feel whole, and he didn't want to stop here.

He leaned back against the pool wall, Amelie in his arms. The music had died. Wind rattled and the waves boomed louder.

Rain squiggled down the panes. Steam rose softly around them.

He'd fallen, hard and fast, for this unusual, vital young woman who'd inserted herself into his life. And she'd given him a gift—she'd come into his cold, dark, walled-off world of self-absorbed loss and grief, and she'd reached out a hand, a bridge, showing him a way back from the cliff edge.

Yet a distant caution whispered inside Tariq. He still had to hear from Omair. It would be morning in the States now. Maybe word had already come. Maybe Omair was trying to call him right now. But as he held her, he felt she was true. Real. He'd felt the care in her touch, seen it in her eyes. These things weren't lies.

"Amelie?"

She looked up at him.

He wanted to say thank you, but couldn't seem to articulate it in a way that didn't seem trite. She had no idea what she'd done for him. His eye filled with emotion.

"You only cry with one eye," she said, reaching up to wipe a tear that had escaped down his right cheek. His chest clutched. He felt exposed, then slowly he smiled.

"Yeah," he said. "The tear ducts were damaged on the other side."

She returned his smile and his heart almost hurt with the sight of it. "Why are you upset?"

"I'm not. You've made me exquisitely happy. I've been known to tear up at the sound of an exquisite cello composition—it's a release."

A strange look crossed her features. She hooked her bare leg over his, leaned her head against his chest. Then she said, "I've never been with a man who'll admit something like that. Especially such a powerful man."

Tariq inhaled deeply. He needed to come clean with her—wanted to. Now. But he had to speak to Omair first, and Zakir. His secret was theirs, too. His coming out would require new strategy in regards to the throne. And The Moor.

"Will you get a glass one?"

Her question distracted him.

"A glass what?" he said.

"Eye."

"Should I?"

"I don't know—I like the patch. It gives you a dangerous air." She laughed, and his smile deepened, pulling stiffly into the left side of his face, farther than it had gone before. And it felt good.

"I also like that you smile with one half of your face."

"My brothers say I should've had plastic surgery."

"Yet you didn't."

"No," he said thoughtfully. "I didn't care." He looked down into her eyes. "Until now."

She swallowed, a current of something moving behind her eyes. His gaze lowered to her full, creamy breasts, buoyant in the water.

"You're beautiful, Amelie." He touched her cheek. "In so many ways. You've reminded me what's important." Duty, family. An ancient code of desert justice. The need to find The Moor and fight back, not be beaten down by him. "Thank you," he whispered.

She took his crippled hand in hers, lacing her fingers through his. And in that moment Tariq loved her. Wholly, if that was possible. Perhaps it was just the lust talking, the afterglow of good sex.

His gaze went to their entwined hands underwater. And he noticed a tiny medallion glimmering like a golden sun against the black-pearl surface of the pool.

He reached in, picked it up, held it out on his palm.

She made a soft sound, her hand going to her neck. "My chain! It must've broken."

But Tariq's attention was transfixed by the medallion resting against his hand. The gold had been fashioned into the image of the sun and it was superimposed by a jambiya—a traditional, curved Arabic dagger. Ice hardened around his heart.

He looked slowly up into her eyes. She was watching him, a strange look in her features. And Tariq's entire world tilted. Even the light in the pool room seemed to change as the wind suddenly screamed shrill and high in the turrets and rain lashed with renewed force against the abbey windows.

All the warmth, affection, desire—every good thing he'd felt about this naked woman in front of him turned sour, dark. Cold. Sharp.

"Who *are* you?" His words came out hoarse.

Blood drained from her face. Her mouth went slack for a moment.

"What…do you mean?"

"I said, who are you?"

Confusion twisted through her face, her eyes beginning to gleam, her nose going pink at the tip.

"I…I was going to tell you, Tariq. I—"

"Tariq!" A black rage rose inside him. "You knew all along who I was!"

A wild desperation entered her big eyes. "Please, hear me out. I came here tonight to tell you that I—"

The rage exploded like shrapnel through his chest. "Tell me *what?* That you're my enemy, that you work for a terrorist organization? That you've come to finish off what your people started on the tarmac at JFK? Just *when* were you going to tell me this?" he demanded. "*After* you made me dinner? *After* you seduced and screwed me?"

He surged up out of the water, stood naked and dripping over her.

"Was that what this was?" He waved his hand between their bodies. "Were you sent to sleep with me, to get something out of me?"

She went sheet white. Emotion pooled into her eyes. His rage festered, curdling with the bitterness of betrayal.

He grabbed a towel, threw it at her.

"Get out."

"Tariq, please, listen to me, that's not—"

"I said, get out."

He went to a console on the wall, pressed the intercom button, his gaze not leaving her for an instant. "I want two men standing guard outside the pool room door," he ordered into the intercom. "Make sure they're armed."

She stood slowly up as he spoke, a naked Venus rising from his whirlpool, water sliding luminous down creamy skin, her curls slicked back from her face, her lips swollen from his kisses. Breasts high and rounded, nipples dusky against pale flesh, the delta of hair between her thighs dark, wet. A spy—a traitor. Who'd made him feel, helped him come back to life, then dashed it all like waves on the rocks below.

All lies.

"Cover yourself," he barked. The sight of her nakedness, her beauty, was fuelling a dangerous feeling of violence in him. He wanted to lash out at her, physically hurt her for not being the woman she'd claimed to be.

She bent down, picked up the towel, wrapped it around her torso, her knuckles white. She shot a glance at the door.

"Don't even think about leaving here," he growled at her.

The wind screamed, like the sound of a dying woman, a ghost in pain.

She came toward him.

"Don't." He pointed his clawed fingers at her. "Do not come near me. Do not—" Emotion rode rough through his chest, strangling the words in his throat. Goddamn it, he'd fallen hard for her. He *wanted* her to be Amelie, to be real, true.

He fisted his good hand around the medallion, then threw it at her bare feet. "What did you think—that I wouldn't *see* this?"

"Tariq, please, I don't know what you're talking about."

"Did he send you himself, or are you working under orders from one of his cells?"

A raw fear entered her face now. "Who? *What* cells?"

He jerked his chin to the gold medallion. "You wear the mark of the Sun Clan."

She looked confused.

"The mark of The Moor," he said, his blood pounding. "The symbol of MagMo."

Her jaw dropped in shock.

A tiny lick of disquiet flicked through him at the sight of the surprise on her face.

"You're actually trying to tell me you don't know what this symbol stands for, where it comes from?" he said.

"I don't."

"That image of a sun and jambiya was once tattooed onto the lower backs of the princes of the Sun Clan, an ancient Saharan tribe that went to battle with the Al Arif bedouins thousands of years ago, a battle that was said to have resulted in the creation of the Kingdom of Al Na'Jar. And that image—" he pointed at it "—is now worn in medallion form by MagMo operatives, terrorists who've sworn allegiance to a man known only as The Moor, a man using ancient desert history to create war in my country. He wants to take over our kingdom for himself. He wants our oil. And he wants power."

"The medallion is not mine," she snapped, an anger building in her.

He barked a harsh laugh.

"My name is Bella DiCaprio," she said. "*That's* what I was going to tell you."

Something inside him stilled at her words. Yet Bella could see muscles bulging at his neck and his hooked, dark features were etched with rage. He stood in front of her, looking more powerful naked than clothed. And the violence that seemed to be simmering just under his skin terrified her.

"I'm a journalist from Washington, D.C.," she said, words coming quickly now, before he erupted. "I came to the island for a story. I believed you were alive, living here in the abbey, that the palace lied about your death. And I—"

"A *story!*" He spat the words out as if they were foul in his mouth.

Bella closed her eyes, digging for strength. There was no right way—no easy way—to say this anymore. "Not just a story," she said. "This is not just about you anymore. It's bigger. It's…"

She heard men outside the door, their voices loud. The door was flung open. One entered, but Tariq didn't bother to look at him. His attention remained solely on Bella as he issued a curt command to his man in Arabic.

The man retreated, closing the door behind him. She heard the lock turn.

And she knew she was trapped. In a cold haunted abbey on a cliff, armed men outside the door. And only Hurley, Scoob and Agnes knew where she was.

"I used to work for the *Washington Daily,*" she said, her voice quivering, and she hated herself for showing fear. "I covered stories on you, Tariq, after the bombing at JFK."

Hatred flashed in his eye and his fist balled as if he was struggling to hold his rage in. This was not the broken specter of a man she'd first glimpsed in the mist along the cliff edge. She didn't know this person in front of her at all. This was a new Tariq, a savage side to him she'd not glimpsed in her research.

Cold fear crawled deeper into her.

"I was there, at the airport with a photographer when the blast occurred. We were covering a separate story when it happened. The photographer was Derek Jones. My boyfriend. I... " She broke his gaze, unable to hold the intensity. She looked instead at the medallion in a puddle of water near her feet. "That part was all true. Everything I told you about my boyfriend, my family, that was all me. The *real* me." She looked up, steeled her jaw at the expression on his face.

"We covered the bombing from an eyewitness perspective, and then the *Daily* let me run with the story as things continued to develop over the following months. I covered your life, your history, your background, Tariq. I felt like I knew you, I—"

"You do *not* know me! You know *nothing* about my family, or what we are capable of in the face of deception." She inhaled, shaky.

I fell in love with you before I even came here...

She wanted to tell him that. She wanted to make him understand that she cared for him with a passion even she didn't fully comprehend. That he'd become an obsession, dominated her life. That she'd put everything on the line to come here and find him, to tell his story.

It sunk in now, as she faced him. It was just that—an obsession. And she felt suddenly like a little girl who'd worshiped her hero, a sheik, a dark prince, from afar, imagining things that were not possible. She felt like little orphan Bella again. A cast-off who couldn't make it in the big time.

She swallowed hard against the ball of failure and reality ballooning in her throat.

He started to speak.

"No, please, Tariq, let me just finish." But her voice came out thin now. "The *Daily* laid me off a few months ago. Budget cuts. Derek escaped the ax because he was sleeping with the boss's daughter. I found this out the very same day my position was terminated—that was all true." She spoke as fast as she could, fighting the emotion that threatened to engulf her voice, fighting time to get her message across before he did something rash.

"I ended up writing a blog for a website called Watchdog. In my various posts I took Senator Sam Etherington to task as I followed his presidential campaign—something I'd also been doing for the *Daily*. At the same time, while your family claimed you were dead, I just couldn't drop the story on you. It didn't feel finished. The tiny news release from the palace felt wrong, false. So did the private funeral. I mean, you'd been engaged for two years and were about to be married and none of your fiancée's family were even there. So I...I called Julie Belard's father."

"You did *what?*" His face twisted at mention of Julie's name, as if she was fouling something sacred.

"I did what journalists do, Tariq. I started digging. Ambassador Belard told me about Julie's love of this island and the abbey, how you used to come here with her for the opera festival. Then with help from a computer expert I learned your family corporation had actually bought the abbey."

Sweat beaded along Bella's lip. She clutched her towel tighter across her chest. "From D.C. I called the travel agent here on the Ile-en-Mer, and he told me the owner, an injured foreigner, moved into the abbey in August, the same month the palace said you'd died. The travel agent said you were living as a recluse, and had closed off the abbey to the public. The timing, everything about your injuries… I believed it *had* to be you.

"My colleagues helped me create an alias, and I spent part of my severance package to come here. That's why I was taking photos of you on the cliff."

She stood, shaking, edgy, feeling as if bared for judgment now that she'd spoken her truth.

He took a slow step toward her. She flinched inside, fighting the urge to step back.

"You came all this way, went to all this trouble, to *expose* me?" Disdain, disgust, entered his features. "You came to wreck my life, profit from of my loss, my grief. You stood there listening to me talking about my fiancée and my accident all the while knowing everything about me."

She lifted her chin. "It's not just about you. I found a photo of you online, posing with Dr. Alexis Etherington at a medical convention in Chicago years ago."

Blood drained under his dark complexion.

"I posted it on my blog."

"Why?" A muscle pulsed fast at his neck. She swallowed, nervous about venturing into more dangerous territory, of including others in his family.

"Partly an attempt to solicit information," she said quietly. "It worked. I got an anonymous tip." She hesitated. "The tip came from Althea Winston, the wife of a man named Travis Johnson who was shot and killed in an underground parking lot in D.C. a few months ago. He worked for a company called Strategic Alliances. A man named Benjamin Raber was his boss."

Recognition flickered in his eyes.

"Do you know any of this?"

"Go on." His order was curt.

She cleared her throat. "Althea Winston implied Strategic Alliances was a front for a U.S. black ops hit unit called STRIKE, and that her husband had been ordered by Raber to have your brother, Omair, assassinated."

His face changed. He reached quickly for a towel, tying it around his waist.

"Continue."

"It appears presidential candidate Senator Sam Etherington might have blackmailed Raber to make this happen. We've been gathering proof."

"*What* proof?"

She was silent.

"Amelie—"

"Bella," she reminded him.

He inhaled sharply.

But before he could speak again, she said, "After Althea Winston tipped me off, she was run off a bridge. She and her daughter were killed. My own apartment was ransacked, and I was attacked in an alley by three men wearing balaclavas. Two of the men, at least, spoke Arabic. In defending myself, I ripped that medallion from one of the men's necks." She pointed at the piece of gold on the floor.

He angled his head. Disbelief in his face. "You didn't give it to the police? You just decided to wear it yourself, like some trophy?"

"I didn't trust anyone. Do you honestly think I'd have worn that in front of you if I knew what it was? I didn't know my attackers were MagMo operatives. I initially thought they were Sam's people, trying to keep the existence of STRIKE hidden, trying to hide the fact he attempted to assassinate a royal from what's supposed to be an allied country. I also thought they could even be your people."

"*My* people?"

"I didn't know why you were hiding, or what lengths your family would go to keep a secret. Or what really went down with Omair, or if he was even still alive."

"They're working together," he said, very quietly. "MagMo and STRIKE. At least as far as Omair was concerned. The Moor wants us all dead. STRIKE appears to be attempting to fulfill his wish."

Adrenaline exploded in her veins.

"You *know* this—for certain?" she said.

"We know Johnson was ordered to have Omair assassinated, and we know that whoever gave Johnson the order was working in alliance with MagMo in North Africa. We didn't know the order could have come from Sam Etherington."

"Even though the queen of Al Na'Jar is Sam's ex?"

He went dead still. "I don't know what you're talking about."

"Tariq," she said quietly, "in my bag in the kitchen is a family photograph I took from your wallet. I recognized Nikki as Alexis from that old Chicago medical convention photo taken with you, the one I posted on my blog. To be certain, I had the image run through sophisticated biometrics software. I know your brother's wife is Sam's ex."

He reached instantly for the intercom, barked another order.

Within seconds his butler entered the room, and handed him Bella's sling bag. Rummaging through it, Tariq removed the photo.

"Who else has seen this?" His words were clipped, ice cold.

"My colleagues at the Watchdog site. They ran a copy through the biometrics software, then they shredded it."

"Shredded?"

"Hackers have been trying to get into the Watchdog system—we think it's Etherington's people. The photo is in my bag because I was going to give it back to you tonight. I started to tell you everything in the kitchen, but…" Her voice faded.

The fact they'd made love—that sex had distracted both of them—hung fresh and tangible between them.

"What are your colleagues' names?"

She remained silent, unwilling to endanger Hurley, Scoob, Agnes.

He regarded her for several beats. Wind screamed louder, rising, falling, as it whipped through the ancient stone turrets, a banshee, a warning, a desperate cry for help thrown over the island. Then he held up the photo. "This," he said quietly, "*this* cannot get out. No matter what."

She swallowed.

"Now, tell me what proof you have that Sam Etherington is behind the STRIKE attempt to kill my brother."

She flattened her mouth. She didn't have the kind of proof he wanted, not yet—but if Tariq thought she had some kind of irrefutable evidence that Sam Etherington tried to kill his brother, if he wanted something badly enough from her, she had a negotiating tool. It might keep her alive.

"And where will that leave me, if I give my proof?"

"You're never going to tell this story, Bella, so you might as well cooperate."

"And just how do you plan to stop me from telling it?"

He vibrated with anger.

"Nikki can have nothing, I repeat, *nothing* to do with this! That is my brother's wish. It's my family's wish. It's something I will defend to the death."

"Why?"

"Because Sam tried to kill her, and if he finds she's alive, he *will* try again. And that, Bella, is why you're not going anywhere, and why you're not going to break this story. I will not allow my indiscretion, my failure to recognize you for what you are, to harm my family."

She barely heard the rest of his words. So it was true— the senator *had* tried to murder his wife. This was going to change the face of the election, of U.S. politics. And if Etherington really was behind a black ops assassin squad operating on foreign soil without permission, it could change the face of international relations. This was monstrous. She had to get out of here, break this news.

"Why did the senator want his wife dead?" she asked quietly.

"He was having an affair. Nikki—Alexis—found out. She was going to sue for custody of the kids, expose Sam for what he was. But he was up for a Senate seat and firm on family values. He didn't want this out, he didn't want to lose his bid for the Senate, and he didn't want to lose his kids, so he hired a hit man to run her off the bridge. Except the man he hired didn't know Sam's twins were in the backseat at the time, and they were killed instead of his wife. Sam then went about systematically destroying an innocent, intelligent, strong, beautiful physician—driving her into the depths of grief and despair. But she survived. She went to Africa under an assumed name and worked illegally as a nurse in a remote mission, and when she inadvertently crossed the border into Al Na'Jar while trying to save some orphans, she met Zakir. She is now married to my brother. She saw him into his blindness. She is his guiding light, his eyes, and he will do *anything* to protect her, to keep her from being dragged through that sordid past history. That is why we will never use Nikki to go after Sam. *That* is why we need your proof that he was behind Omair's assassination attempt."

Bella remained silent, energy pulsing through her body at this revelation.

He swung round abruptly, marched toward the door.

"This is not just about *your* family, Tariq!" she called after him.

Slowly, he turned.

"It's a story the U.S. electorate *needs* to know," she said. "My country is going to the polls in a few months and in all likelihood are going to put a very sick man into power. If Etherington tried to have Omair killed, he also likely conspired to murder Travis Johnson, Althea Winston and their innocent five-year-old daughter. The reason I came up here tonight was to return your photo, confess everything and ask for your cooperation, your side of the story. Please, Tariq, talk to me, tell me what *you* know. Tell me why you think Etherington might be colluding with operatives from the same terrorist organization that almost killed your brother—help me tell *that* story. We can work together."

He stared at her in disgust.

"You're a cheap thief and a liar. You slept with me for your own gain. Like some muckraker, some bottom-feeder, you came here under false pretences to blow apart my life, to drag my brother's wife back into the worst nightmare of her past." He raised his hooked hand, pointed it at her. "What makes it worse, what makes me sick, is I *fell* for you. I *enabled* you."

Tears burned into in her eyes. She glowered at him, shivering from cold and stress.

"You deceived me, too, Tariq. You made love to me under an alias, too."

He glowered at her. Then said, "Tell me what proof you have on Sam, then maybe we can talk."

"How can I trust you'll let me go if I do?"

His mouth flattened, his scars more vicious, sinister. "You can't."

"Then I can't tell you."

Grabbing her bag, he turned his back on her, rapped hard once on the door.

The lock turned and the door opened.

"I'm not a muckraker!" she yelled suddenly behind him. He stilled, hand on door handle. But this time he did not turn to face her.

"I gambled everything on this story because I'm a damn good reporter! I saw the potential of this, I dug up the clues—and the truth now needs to be told in the interests of national security! I almost got killed for this story. Others *did* die. And I feel responsible for their deaths. I owe this to them, too!"

She felt spent suddenly. "It's all I have... I *need* this story, Tariq. And you have no damn right to call me a bottom-feeder. I don't have royal coffers, a family, an army that can bail me out. I don't have a job. I don't have anyone—I've got only myself."

She saw the muscles across his back tighten.

"One thing you don't do, Bella, is threaten my family," he said without looking at her. Then he stepped out the door.

She rushed up to him. "Where are you going!"

His bodyguard moved in, blocked her, said in French, "You're staying in the pool room."

The door *thucked* shut. The lock turned.

She rattled the handle. "You can't keep me prisoner!" She banged. Silence. Just the mournful wail of the wind. "You can't lock me up in here!"

Bella turned, cursed and slid down the door to the floor. Tears burned and spilled silent and angry down her face. She'd lost him.

She had no phone, no way of contacting anyone. And he sure as hell wasn't going to let her tell her story.

Everything she'd fought for these past months was gone.

Perhaps even her life.

Chapter 9

Tariq punched in Omair's number, agitated by the violence he'd felt toward Bella. He'd wanted to punish her for not being Amelie, for not being the woman he'd been falling in love with. For daring him to hope, when all she wanted was to destroy him with a story. And still, he didn't know if what she'd just revealed back in the pool room was the real truth. For all he knew she could still be working with MagMo, pulling the wool over his eyes.

He'd been a bloody fool. He'd allowed her to blind him, seduce him, so thoroughly she could steal from his wallet right under his nose, and find a photo of Nikki. His own stupidity and carelessness had almost cost Nikki her anonymity, her freedom from her past, and put his family at risk.

"Tariq," Omair said crisply as he answered. "Where've you been? I've been trying to reach you for the last two hours. There *is* no Amelie Chenard. She's an imposter, a journalist from D.C. Her real name is Bella DiCaprio."

Tariq's fist tightened around the phone. "Is it true, can you verify her ID?"

"You *know?*"

"She confessed. We need to talk about her claims, but first, tell me what you have on her. I want to be sure."

"Bella DiCaprio worked with the *Washington Daily* until she was laid off some months ago. She'd been covering stories on you ever since the blast at JFK. She was on site when it happened, with a photographer named Derek Jones who shot what became that famous photo of you racing from the burning jet with Julie in your arms."

Tariq closed his eyes.

I covered your life, your history, your background, Tariq. I felt like I knew you...

He tried to take a slow breath.

"According to my investigator, DiCaprio was born in Chicago, abandoned by an unknown mother at an inner-city hospital and finally adopted out of the system at the age of three."

So it was true.

"Italian-American mother and father, five biological sons."

Everything I said about my boyfriend, my family...that was all me. That part was true...

"She studied at Chicago University, majored in journalism and political studies, worked at several smaller newspapers before taking her job with the *Daily*. After she was laid off she started a blog with a group called Watchdog. Filed a police report about an attack last month. Then she went missing."

"And showed up here," Tariq finished.

So everything she'd said about herself in the pool room was honest. Real. And that mattered to him on a level he wasn't willing to articulate to himself, or truly acknowledge. Not now.

Tariq told Omair what Bella had claimed about Sam Etherington, STRIKE, Raber, Johnson and his wife, Althea.

"She said Sam Etherington is behind the attempt to kill you. Which means he's also behind the attempt to kill Faith."

"And you say she has proof?"

"She says she does, but she's not giving it."

"We need to force her." Omair's words were sharp. "I'll do it. I'll leave at once by jet for Paris, then helo to Ile-en-Mer. I'll bring some men. Keep her locked up, don't say a thing to her until I get there, understand?"

A raw protective instinct rose unexpected and powerful in Tariq. Omair was a skilled—and sometimes lethal—interrogator. He was known in certain circles for his ability to make anyone talk, but some of his methods turned Tariq's stomach. He didn't want Omair anywhere near her—especially since what he was going to say next could seal Bella's fate when it came to his brothers.

"There's more," he said quietly. "She knows Nikki is Alexis."

Silence swelled between them.

"How?" Omair said.

"She found a family photo in my wallet and recognized Alexis from an old medical convention photo. Bella had her colleagues run it through facial-recognition software."

Another beat of silence. Then a sharp curse in Arabic.

"Nikki *has* to stay out of this."

"I fear Nikki is central to all of this," Tariq said quietly. "Think about it, Omair. If Sam was behind the STRIKE order to assassinate you, then it's Sam who is in collusion with MagMo. And who in MagMo wants the entire Al Arif family dead? The Moor. Why on earth would Sam help The Moor—he's a terrorist, an enemy of the United States."

"Because The Moor must have something in turn that will destroy Sam," Omair said quietly.

"Exactly," Tariq said. "It *has* to be. I think The Moor has somehow found out about Nikki, and he's using her existence to blackmail the next president of the United States into helping him. And if that's true, then Sam already knows where Nikki is."

"Then why hasn't he acted? Why hasn't he come after Nikki already?"

"Maybe he *is* coming after her. Maybe that's where this collusion is going. The one thing The Moor wants most is control over our kingdom and our oil. If he's managed to blackmail Sam into promising U.S. military backing of a coup in Al Na'Jar once he's in the White House, we're toast. And then, when The Moor takes control of our kingdom, Sam gets the oil deal and Middle Eastern allies he's been promising in his campaign—"

"And Nikki and Zakir are killed in the coup," Omair said. "Sam's problem is gone. His ex-wife dies as do any potential allegations of murder, or potential for further blackmail."

"Exactly," said Tariq. "The Moor already thinks you and I are both dead. Zakir and Nikki—they're his last target. And this is all about her."

Omair inhaled deeply on the other end of the line, then said, "Listen, Tariq, if Bella really does have irrefutable proof Sam used STRIKE to try and kill me, and that he conspired to have Johnson and his family murdered, we can use that proof to nail him without ever involving Nikki. We can stop this before it even touches her. We *have* to get that information. Hold her securely until I get there."

"And then?" Tariq's voice was cold.

"Then when she's given us the proof, she's free to go. Sam will no longer be a threat to Nikki if he's behind bars for murder."

"And what do you think is going to happen when you finally let Bella free and she goes to the police, tells them we forcibly confined her, interrogated her?"

Very quietly, Omair said, "We have diplomatic immunity, Tariq. And you'll come home, of course, lay low in Al Na'Jar."

Tariq cursed bitterly.

"Look, whatever has happened between you two, remember this. She got into your house, into your head, into your bed and into your wallet, for a reason. A story. To expose our family, and profit from it. She's an opportunist, and a devious one."

Tariq raked his hand over his hair and turned to stare at the rain shimmering down the black windows in his office. Outside the night was icy cold, blustery.

"Hold her until I get there," Omair reiterated. "I'm on my way."

"No," Tariq insisted quietly, but firmly. "This has to end. All of it. We'll use Bella in another way. I'll talk to her, get her to cooperate with me. I'll tell her that she's free to go and break her story, taking Sam down with whatever proof she claims she has. *But* I will request she leave the Nikki-Alexis angle out. And I'll tell her why—I'll let her know what terrible hell Nikki has been through to get where she is, to simply survive. In exchange I let Bella reveal my whereabouts, the fact I'm alive. She can run my photo, use my comments. And I give her what we know about STRIKE, from your and Faith's angle, without revealing names."

"The Moor will come after you."

"Then let him. I'll be waiting."

Silence.

"And if she doesn't agree? If she reneges—how can you be sure she'll keep her word?"

"She's a decent person, Omair. I feel she'll agree. And if we don't go this route, if we don't try and manage what we can of the story, someone else will expose Nikki, eventually. Already three people have seen that photo—"

"Who!"

"Bella's colleagues from Watchdog."

"What are their names?" His tone was clipped, cold. Tariq knew the sound well—his brother was in soldier mode, assassin mode.

"I don't know their names, and you can't do anything about it, Omair—it's already out of our control. Bella said hackers had been trying to get into the Watchdog servers. If they did, the information about Nikki could be in anyone's hands by now. I'm going to call Zakir. He needs to prepare Nikki, just in case. Meanwhile I'm going to talk to Bella."

"Tariq," Omair warned darkly. "Do *not* talk to her until I arrive. Do you understand—"

Tariq hung up, a new kind of anger humming through his veins. Not only had Bella betrayed him, she'd now driven a wedge between him and his brothers.

Hurley blinked through the hot blood leaking into his eyes. The gash on his head was bleeding badly. He'd lost track of time. The warehouse was dark, cold. His breathing was shallow and he struggled to take in air through his crushed nose. Blood pooled in his throat, gagging him. His ribs felt as though they'd been broken. On the other side of the warehouse Agnes was strapped to a metal chair, hands tied behind her back, head slumped forward. Her red-framed cat-eye glasses lay crushed at her bare feet.

Blood trickled down her leg where her skin had been sliced repeatedly with a razor.

A tall, dark-skinned man in a ski mask held a Taser against the translucent skin at Agnes's throat. But this time she remained limp, no longer responsive. Fear roared through Hurley's chest.

"One last time," the man said, as he pressed the Taser into her neck. "Where is she? Where did Bella DiCaprio take those photos of Tariq Al Arif?"

Agnes moaned, muttering something.

No, Agnes, no! The words screamed to come out of Hurley, but he couldn't voice them. Not this time. He didn't want them to hurt Agnes any more than they already had. At the same time, he knew the minute she gave them what they wanted, it would be over for both of them. It was up to Bella now. If she could break the story before these men found and stopped her—if she could expose Sam Etherington before he got into power…it might at least be worth something.

The man fired the Taser into Agnes' neck, and her body spasmed as she screamed.

"Bastards!" he spluttered through broken lips trying to lunge forward in his chair, wire cutting into his bound wrists. "Leave her al—"

A crack blew through the back of his skull as the man behind struck him with an iron bar. Hurley felt his head crush inward as light and pain sparked through his eyes. His world went black.

Seventeen minutes later, Aban Ghaffar's encrypted satellite phone rang in his Manhattan penthouse. He was lying naked on his massage table, a nice view of the skyline through his tinted, floor-to-ceiling windows. His masseuse worked a muscle in his buttock that had been troubling him after his last ski trip—she had good fingers, strong fingers. He lifted his head slightly and reached for the phone on the table at his side.

"Yes?" he said.

He listened carefully, killed the call then hit the number for his son in Paris. As the phone rang, Aban felt a familiar spark of resentment—once again Amal had not managed to live up to expectations. He had not found out what financial interests the Al Arif corporation held on the coast of France, nor had he managed to zero in on a location for Tariq Al Arif. But his team in D.C. had come through. Aban now had another chance to test his son. A male heir was imperative to his culture. Someone would have to carry this legacy forward one day. He hoped his boy was going to rise to the job.

Amal answered in Paris.

"Ile-en-Mer," Aban said quietly. "It's an island off the Brittany coast. He is in the Mont Noir Abbey on the west cliffs. She is working as a maid for a woman named Estelle Dubois who lives on the village side of the island. DiCaprio is staying in maid's quarters on the Dubois property."

He hung up, closed his eyes, feeling the masseuse's hands work higher, the oil warm as it was rubbed into his skin. He took some measure of comfort in the fact Amal and his men would be on the move within minutes, a private chopper and pilot at their disposal. It would be a mere matter of hours before DiCaprio was silenced, and Tariq properly, and finally, disposed of.

Omair was already gone. Princess Dalilah would be taken care of during the coup. She was not in line to inherit the throne, so not a pressing problem, but she was a dynamic young woman with powerful connections in New York and around the world. She had the power to rouse resistance to him. She, too, would eventually need to be silenced.

When the time was right.

Like a caged animal, Bella paced in front of the dark pool room windows. She'd changed into her clothes and she'd been through the gym, the showers, the sauna, the locker room—the entire place, rattling doors, looking for vents, trying to find a way out.

Panic clawed through her.

You're never going to tell this story, Bella...

What, exactly, did that mean?

Sam tried to kill Nikki, and if he finds she's alive, he will try again. And that, Bella, is why you're not going anywhere, and you're not going to break this story...

That was exactly why she *had* to break this story.

She needed to get to a phone, tell Hurley and the others that her alias was blown, that she was in danger. The world needed to hear this about Etherington. She had a duty to get it out there, tell what she knew.

Anxiety mounted in her. It was still raining outside, still windy. Still dark.

She didn't have a watch on—no idea of the time.

Ripples, soft, suddenly flowed over the interior surface of the pool as outside a sharp blast of wind hit the windows. She spun round as it dawned on her—the wind on the water outside was causing the ripples *inside*. She went to the edge of the pool where the water flowed under glass. The air coming beneath the glass was cool. She put her hands into the water. Her fingertips touched a metal security grid under the surface. She glanced up. This was an indoor-outdoor pool—there had to be a way of operating that grid, moving it aside so swimmers could move through from this end of the pool to the outside water.

Bella lurched to her feet, whirled round, scanning the room. Then she saw it—a small metal cabinet set into the far wall. She hurried over, tried to yank the cabinet door open.

Locked.

Frustration bit into her. She ran into the gym, pulled one of the pins out of a stack of weights, and rushed back. Using the pin, Bella rammed and pried open the cabinet door.

She flicked the switch.

Slowly the grate moved aside. She had a way out of the pool room. But then what?

Eight-foot-high spiked walls surrounded the estate. There were security cameras watching the gates. She'd never get out without tripping some alarm. She dragged her hands over her hair in frustration, her brain racing. She recalled suddenly the sedan she'd seen in the converted stables when she'd gone looking for Kiki who'd escaped from the kitchen garden. One of Tariq's men had been polishing the sedan, another vacuuming the interior, doors open. Bella remembered there'd been a remote resting on the dash. And on the garage wall nearby there was a board with keys.

Perhaps the keys for the car would be on that board.

Or maybe, if she could access the remote, she could use it to open the main gates without triggering an alarm.

Bella thought of Tariq's men, their flat, dark eyes, their weapons. Her heart hammered and fear twisted through her as she glanced at the black water flowing through to the outdoors.

It was almost freezing outside, more snow in the forecast. Even if she did get out of the main gates without alerting anyone, she'd have wet clothes, and she'd still need to get down the mountain to the village. Hypothermia would set in before that happened.

Bella went back into the gym and found what she was looking for—a garbage bag inside an empty trash can. Quickly, she undressed and stuffed her clothes and boots into the bag. Pressing her knees into the bag to squash the air out and vacuum-pack her clothes as best she could, she tied double knots. If she was quick going under, her clothes would stay dry.

She wrapped a towel around her body, ran out to the water.

Bella shot a glance at the door. It was now or never. She dropped the towel, slid into the pool, dragging her garbage bag of clothes with her and thanked the Lord the water was heated. Taking a deep breath, Bella dived under, pulling the buoyant bag with her as she held her breath and swam beneath the windows.

She broke the surface on the other side. Cold wind slammed her face. The sky was pitch black and low with clouds, rain driving down, the infinity pool giving the impression of nothing but a fall of water disappearing over cliffs to the smashing waves below. Bella swam to the closest edge, pulled herself out and ducked behind rocks out of sight from the windows. Fingers going numb, she tore open the trash bag. Her hair felt like ice against her cheeks.

She wriggled into her clothes and pulled on her boots. Her next goal was to get to Madame's house and her laptop, or to a phone—Tariq had taken her prepaid cell with her bag.

Pushing wet hair back from her face, she ran round the side of the abbey, accessing the converted stable area from the back.

It was dead silent, no one in sight.

Bella moved in the shadows toward the sedan, peered in the windows. The remote was still there, on the dash. And hanging on the board she found a set of keys that matched the sedan model. Bella said a silent prayer of thanks before carefully, quietly, pushing open the massive wooden stable doors. One of the doors groaned, and she stilled, heart jackhammering, but the wind and rain were drowning out sound.

Climbing into the driver's seat, Bella tried to catch her breath and think straight. Once she opened those gates and drove through, they'd see her on camera. She'd have to drive fast once she was clear of those gates.

Filling her lungs with a deep breath, she started the ignition. Then she put the car in gear, and slowly she drove through the stable doors, heading for the gates.

The man in the security room watching the camera footage glanced up.

The sedan was leaving the abbey grounds. He noted the time and returned his attention to his newspaper. It was not unusual for the car to leave at odd hours, with the staff running errands for the boss.

Tariq leaned back in his chair. Closing his eyes, he rubbed his neck where damaged muscles were beginning to ache. It was almost 2:00 a.m. and the strain of reading was giving him a headache.

His chef had long ago taken Bella's burned roast from the oven, tossed it in the garbage, and staff had cleared away table settings for two. Tariq had kept two guards stationed outside the pool room door.

Bella's image sifted into his mind—her naked skin, pale against his, her eyes luminous as she'd straddled him, rocked against him. His pulse quickened as he thought of how he'd found her in the kitchen. She'd seemed so vital. There'd been something so basic and invigorating about the kitchen, too, the scents, the warmth, the steam—the center of hearth and home. And she'd been at the core of it all.

He recalled the way her eyes had locked on to his when she'd seen him standing silent in the doorway.

At that moment Tariq had wanted nothing more than Amelie. To take her in that kitchen, right in that cauldron of warmth and sustenance, to be someone he'd stopped being a long, long time ago.

But then, just when he'd been lured to that tipping point between past, present and future, just when he was beginning to think that not only had he found himself again, but maybe he'd found something better…he'd found it was all a lie.

Tariq breathed in deep, returned to reading online the stories Bella had written about him, about his family, his country, its politics. Her stories on Sam Etherington. The senator's campaign promises.

The more Tariq read, the more he saw the lines between Amelie and Bella blurring. He was beginning to see them as one, the same person.

She *did* care about him, his family—it was evident in her prose. This was not a hack, not a sensationalist. She was a strong writer who questioned everything. And he doubted she earned a penny from the blog, yet she continued to put full effort into her posts.

I'm not a muckraker…I gambled everything on this story because I am a damn good reporter!

He sat back again, thinking of how intimately she must have come to know him through these features, and now, through reading her words, he was getting to know her on a deeper level in turn. This went far beyond lust—the sex they'd shared. This was a powerful emotional connectivity that Tariq could feel, and he was now even more convinced that Bella would come around when she learned what it would mean to his family, what price Nikki would have to pay to be dragged through the media again.

Help me tell this story. We can work together...

He clicked on the image of himself fleeing the wreckage with Julie in his arms, and he winced as it all started to loop afresh through his head. Clenching his jaw, Tariq read the photographer's credit.

Derek Jones.

I was there, at the airport when it happened...with Derek.

The creep who'd hurt her. Tariq believed what Bella had told him about Derek, about her habitually destructive relationships.

Now that his adrenaline had ebbed, he believed that her emotions around her feelings of abandonment, her adoptive parents were genuine, too. He could understand her drive to prove herself.

Glancing at his watch, he got to his feet. Omair would have left Sao Diogo via military jet almost as soon as he'd hung up. He'd be landing in Paris shortly. From Paris he could be on Ile-en-Mer in an hour via chopper, weather permitting.

Tariq needed to get through to Bella before his brother and his F.D.S. colleagues arrived. He could not be responsible for Omair's interrogation techniques. He could not let his brother near this woman who, despite everything, Tariq cared for deeply.

He was going to heal, mend this rift, like the surgeon he was. No violence—not this time. That whole cycle had to end.

Tariq pushed open his study door, moved through the library and made for the pool room. It was almost 3:00 a.m. When he got to the pool room door he asked his men to unlock it and step aside.

He entered, but immediately sensed the place was

empty. The lights were on inside the gym, everything was
eerily quiet.

"Bella?"

His men entered behind him. "Search the area," he commanded.

But she was gone.

One of the men pointed to the underwater security grid.
It had been moved aside. A towel had been dropped at the
side of the pool near the windows.

Tariq spun around—the metal door of the control panel
had been pried open, a weight pin lying on the floor below
it. "Search the grounds!" he barked as he ran toward his
security room. He bust through the door and the man monitoring the bank of screens jerked his head up in surprise.

"Sir?" the man said, lurching to his feet.

"Any breach of perimeter?" demanded Tariq. "She got
out through the pool room—I need to know if she's still
on the estate."

"No, sir, no perimeter breach."

Tariq swiveled around to face the men who'd followed
him. "Then she's still here somewhere. Find her!"

Someone flicked a switch on the control bank and the
external perimeter lights blazed on, illuminating the abbey
grounds in white light.

The man monitoring the screens said suddenly, "Wait,
what if it wasn't a breach? I saw the sedan leave at—" he
glanced at his log "—at 1:38 a.m."

"Sedan?" said Tariq.

"I thought you'd ordered it, sir."

He turned to his men. "Let's go!"

Meanwhile, a dark sedan drove off the private ferry
ramp with a clunk on the southeast side of Ile-en-Mer.

The estates on this side of the island were dark, deserted for the winter.

Amal was at the wheel. Beside him one of his men fiddled with his GPS. The other two men sat in the back. The pilot Amal had contracted was flying a chopper over from the mainland at this very moment, and would be waiting for them to make a quick getaway when they were done— but for now they needed a vehicle to get around the island.

"Turn right at the top of this road," the man with the GPS said.

Their first order of business was find the reporter— Bella DiCaprio. Kill her and her story before Aban lost control over the senator.

Then they would deal with the prince.

Bella slammed on the brakes, put the car in Park. Leaving the door open and engine running, she raced up the pathway, sliding in slush. Using the key Estelle Dubois had left under a mat for her, she let herself into Madame's house. Quieting the dogs she went to the safe, worked the lock, removed her flash drive.

In her room, she opened her computer, booted it up. Hands shaking, terrified Tariq's security men would arrive at any second, she hit the video-call icon for Hurley.

Pick up, pick up, please.

No response.

She tried again, three times, perspiration beading her brow. Still no answer. She bit her lip. Bella quickly retrieved her ID documents, credit card and cash from under the floorboard, dragged her suitcase out from under the bed, began to throw clothes into it, mentally running through the steps to get off the island, into a cab and to Charles de Gaulle airport.

All her clothes in the case, she tried Hurley again.

Still no answer.

But as she closed her suitcase her Skype beeped—incoming call.

Bella swung around. It wasn't Hurley. It was an unknown video caller. She hesitated, then bit the bullet, hit Accept.

Scoob's face filled the screen. The sight of his white, gaunt features, red-rimmed eyes, hair stringier than usual, stopped the breath in Bella's throat as a horrible foreboding feeling sunk through her.

"Scoob?"

"They took him—Hurley. And Agnes. Broke in—"

"*Who?* When!"

"Yesterday. Bella, I can't talk long. They're looking for me now. I arrived seconds after it happened, blood everywhere, computer stuff wrecked. They took them in a van. It—It's bad."

"Did you go to the police?"

"I don't trust *anyone* right now. Listen to me carefully. I managed to clean up the surveillance audio from last summer. I now have copies of Etherington *clearly* talking to Isaiah Gold about colluding with The Moor, and using a STRIKE operative—Faith Sinclair—to take out Omair Al Arif. Once Etherington is elected he will militarily back a coup in Al Na'Jar. In exchange, The Moor's promise is to have Sam's ex, now the queen of Al Na'Jar, killed. He will also deliver oil and Middle East allies to Sam. If Sam does not do these things, The Moor's threat is to reveal the existence of his ex-wife, along with evidence he tried to have her murdered. This guy is as sick as they come."

"You have this *all* on tape?"

"Digital audio file on an external storage device. I put a copy in a safe-deposit box in the Union Bank on Cedar Avenue in Ladysmith, Virginia. Deposit box number is 643.

Do not, I repeat, do *not* write this down. I managed to get the bank manager to hold the key for you and no one else. You'll need ID. I've got another copy on me. I'm going to keep moving, heading west. Go get them, Bella—get the tape, break the story. The audio is the proof you need."

"What about Hurley, Agnes?" Her voice came out a hoarse whisper.

"You can't do anything about them right now. If they got to them, if they made them talk, they're coming after you as we speak, so you better clear the hell out of there, and fast. And…" He closed his eyes, clearly beyond exhausted. "If something happens to me, you're all that's left of Watchdog. Promise me—just promise you'll break this on the blog. For Hurley. For Agnes."

"I swear it."

The icon faded as Scoob logged out.

With shaking hands Bella stuffed her laptop, passport and other documents into a bag and slung it across her chest. Threading her flash drive onto a piece of string, she tied it around her neck and slipped it under her sweater. She grabbed her suitcase and ran out to the idling car.

There was no time for a note for Madame. She threw her suitcase into the back. Foot on the gas, Bella skidded out onto the road and headed for the steep road that switch-backed down to the old harbor. Windshield wipers struggled to keep up with the rain. The dawn was still black, fog thickening the closer she got to the sea.

As she rounded a hairpin bend, Bella swung the wheel too hard and the car fishtailed across wet tarmac, sliding to where the edge of the road dropped off into mountain. She hit the brakes, screeching to a stop. She paused for a moment, heart thumping in her throat.

Stay focused or you will die.

She pulled out again, starting down the mountain just

a little more cautiously. That's when she glimpsed head-lights in her rearview mirror, coming fast.

Tariq's men.

She lay on the gas again, tires squealing round the next hairpin bend.

But the car behind her was coming too fast. It rammed her from the back. Hands fisting on the wheel, Bella strug-gled to control her vehicle.

The car behind her sped up again, this time slamming into her left rear just as she was trying to round the next steep bend. She went into a sickening spin, tires failing to find purchase over the slick surface. Her vehicle caromed against the guardrail, sparks flying. Bella swung her wheel back, trying to make the next bend, but she overshot and went through the next guardrail.

Her car rolled over the edge. Bella's world spiraled into a crunching mess of black sky, branches, rocks, dirt, break-ing glass. The car came to a stop, lolling on its side, the hood bent off, engine whining, the smell of gas strong. Bella lay dead-still for a moment, unable to believe she was alive. Then, cautiously, she tried to move her limbs. Pain radiated out from her shoulder and down her arm as she found her seat belt buckle. She managed to undo it and wriggle her legs free from beneath the crushed dash. The driver's-side window glass had blown out and she was able to drag herself through, pulling her bag with the laptop behind her.

She stood, unsteady on her feet. The treed embankment inclined sharply down toward the harbor in the distance. Rain was coming down heavily now. She could hear men yelling up on the road. Bella caught sight of a flashlight beam panning the darkness up above her. They were com-ing down, looking to see if she'd survived the car wreck. Adrenaline punched through Bella as she started to quickly clamber and slide down the muddy mountain. She came to a stop under the cover of pines and caught her breath. She could taste blood in her mouth. Her lip was cut. So was her hand. Her clothes were ripped.

Another flashlight beam arced through the bushes not far above and Bella heard more yelling. *Arabic*.

Tariq's men weren't just looking for her, they'd tried to kill her, and clearly wanted to finish the job.

She could hear them begin beating brush, widening out from her car, flashlights panning out in circles, voices calling to each other.

Bella started to grope her way down the mountain through trees and brush, clinging onto wet branches where the ground dropped away. Mud sucked at her boots and rocks clattered down where she dislodged them. Brambles ripped at her skin and clothes as she went.

If she could just get down this mountain, make it down to that harbor in the distance… But she stilled as the faint but distinct sound of a helicopter came from somewhere behind the clouds.

She glanced back up the mountain to the road. The headlights of another car panned across the landscape as it rounded a bend. As it approached the first vehicle, Bella heard gunshots.

Quickly, she crouched down into the wet scrub, heart hammering.

Chapter 10

As Tariq and his men rounded a switchback searching for Bella, their path was suddenly blocked by a black sedan stopped sideways across the road, gleaming in the rain, doors wide open. A man standing in front of the car spun round in shock as their lights illuminated him. He was dark-skinned, well-built and tall, with black hair, a goatee, shoulder-length hair.

As if in slow motion, Tariq saw the man raise a gun and take aim. He fired and a hail of bullets exploded across the body of the limousine, several piercing through the windshield, and one traveling so close to Tariq's cheek he could feel the heat and hear it buzz.

"Get down! Automatic weapon!" his driver yelled as he took a hit in his arm and yanked the wheel round, slamming on the brakes. The limo skidded sideways toward the car in the road. The man started to run and yell at someone down the side of the mountain. That's when Tariq saw the damaged guardrail. It looked as though a car had gone through and plunged over the side.

Bella!

Adrenaline rushed through his body as his driver brought the vehicle to a stop. His bodyguards, their own weapons in hand, flung open doors and crouched behind them as they took another burst of gunfire.

One of his men forced Tariq to the floor of the car, but he yelled at his guard to focus on the shooter instead. There were also flashlight beams cutting the blackness—more people down the side of the mountain, making their way back up to the road. They must've been searching for Bella in her car. Had to be MagMo, thought Tariq.

Bella had said she was attacked in D.C. by Arabic-speaking men—that was how she'd come by the medallion. They must have finally traced her here to the island, and they didn't want her breaking her story. He'd bet his life they'd come for him next.

More shots peppered the air as Tariq scrambled into the back of the limo to remove a rifle his men kept in a case.

He got the gun and climbed out the vehicle, crouching behind the door. More bullets pinged off the vehicle and his injured driver returned fire. Rain was coming down heavily now, a silver sheen. The men with flashlights— three of them—were coming back over the edge of the road, running toward their sedan as their comrade covered them. Suddenly, Tariq heard a chopper somewhere above the cloud. He frowned. Omair and his F.D.S. colleagues should be arriving, but they wouldn't be hovering around this side of the island.

"They've got air support coming!" one of his men yelled.

Tariq cursed, ducking back as a bullet smashed through

the window above his head. He reached inside the car for his sat phone, hit speed dial for his brother.

"What are our coordinates!" Tariq yelled to his guard, taking cover behind the passenger door as the phone rang. His guard crawled into the limo passenger seat, staying low, and yelled out the GPS coordinates to Tariq.

Omair answered his phone, the loud noise of the chopper he was in forcing him to yell.

"How far out are you?" Tariq ducked again as more bullets were fired.

"Approaching land, west side of Ile-en-Mer, heading for the abbey landing pad."

"We're on the village side, above harbor, taking enemy fire." Tariq gave the coordinates.

The other chopper was lowering, a powerful searchlight trying to break through the low clouds. They were scanning the mountainside—they must've called it in to help hunt Bella from the air.

Tariq swore, rage exploding through his veins. He got up, balanced the rifle with his bad arm and fired. His men also released a volley of bullets, and the man behind the black sedan took one in the chest, staggered back.

The chopper lowered farther, thudding. Downdraft ripped at trees, whipped mist, drove the rain sideways in squalls.

Suddenly through the cloud cover, an explosion of white light broke through as a searchlight panned over the scene. Someone fired from the chopper. Tariq's men returned the shots, aiming at the craft. The helicopter rose suddenly again, as heavy cloud closed back in. Tariq stepped out from behind the door of his limo, fired again. This time he hit someone. The man stumbled backward, clutching his stomach.

"Cover me!" he yelled to his guards. His men released

another burst of fire as Tariq scrambled behind the limo, then ran to the cliff edge. About fifty yards down was his vehicle, smashed. It had gone through the rail and come to rest against a clump of trees, lying on its side.

He could hear the chopper trying to come in low again. Wind began to rip at his hair, his cloak billowing out behind him from the downdraft.

"Bella!" he screamed down the mountain. "Bella, where are you!"

The lights of the helicopter broke through fog again, the sound reverberating in Bella's bones as the chopper searchlight beamed across the slope once more. She scrambled under a bush and sat dead-still as the spotlight passed right over her, momentarily lighting a narrow and twisting little goat path down the mountain. Her heart kicked. If she used that path, she could get down to the harbor faster. But only if cloud closed in again, because the chopper was going to illuminate her like a sitting duck if she moved out from cover.

Bella crouched farther back into the brambles, shivering from cold, adrenaline, shock. She could hear the ongoing gun battle up on the road, and was chilled as she registered the sound of automatic weapons. She saw lights, heard yelling. But who was fighting who? She'd thought it was Tariq's men after her in that car. Who was in the second vehicle? Who was in the chopper?

A man screamed. More shots. Then more yelling. She saw the chopper coming through cloud again, lowering over the scene on the road above, the searchlights illuminating everything like some kind of mad play. And suddenly she thought, imagined, she heard her name. Bella tried to peer up through the brambles.

She saw him then. Tariq. In a pool of light from the helicopter. Standing way up there on the edge of the road, rifle in hand, his cape billowing out behind him, hair gleaming wet.

"Bella!"

He was calling her. Or was she imagining the sound of his voice in the noise? He began to move off the road, coming down the mountain. Terror gushed through her chest.

She had to get away, from all of them.

She had no idea who to trust, if anyone.

But before she could make a move, Bella saw a man scrambling along the side of the mountain below Tariq. He had a gun. Tariq hadn't seen him coming. The man stopped, aimed his weapon up at the sheik.

A scream of warning rose in Bella's throat. But the vignette went suddenly black as the chopper hovered back into the clouds. She heard another gunshot and Bella shut her eyes tight, bile rising in her throat. She hugged her knees, rocking, wondering if Tariq was dead. Tears streamed down her face. The mud around her ankles was cold. She was hurting. Disoriented. Confused. Her body started to shake. She wasn't going to make it.

Then she thought of Scoob. Of Hurley and Agnes. Of what she'd started, and was now responsible for. She had to move, now, while she could, while it was dark again, while another thick swath of cloud was sifting up from the water.

Bella crawled out from under the bushes. From there she scrambled to where she'd seen the goat path leading down to the sea.

Small waves slapped softly against the ancient stone pier and fog was dense. Bella could barely make out the fishing boats bobbing against their moorings. Faint halos of lamplight lit the length of the pier. She could hear the distant boom of a foghorn.

Staggering along the pier, Bella reached the little ferryman's hut at the end and banged on the door.

It opened. The ferryman was perhaps in his sixties, broad-jawed and whiskered. Her wore a checked shirt and pants with suspenders. Confusion creased his face at the sight of her.

"I...I need a ride to the mainland," she stammered quickly in French. "I must get to the airport in a hurry."

Hand remaining firmly on his doorknob, the ferryman's eyes lowered, taking in her ripped, wet clothing, her cuts, her shaking hands.

"I had an accident on my bike on the way down," she explained. "I'll have to pick up some new clothes at the airport."

He glanced back up the pier in search of her bike.

"Had to leave it...can't be late for my flight." Bella's tongue felt thick. She was having trouble forming words. "Please."

"The fog," he said, "it's thick, the wind off the point is—"

"Please." Desperation cracked her voice. My mother is very ill. I need to get to her. I...I can't let her die without me at her side."

His face softened. "Come, come inside. Wait here." He pulled on a cable-knit sweater and oil slicker as he spoke, then he reached for his oilskin hat, hesitated. "Are you sure you don't want to get dry first?"

"No, no, please. I need to go, now."

He frowned and she could see him wondering if she might be in some kind of trouble, and whether he should inform authorities.

Desperately, Bella reached into her bag, took out the money she'd stashed in the floorboards. "Look, I have cash," she said, holding out a wad. "I'll pay double."

Seconds later the ferryman's little boat was chugging quietly out the harbor, water slick, the mist swirling around them. Beyond the pier the waves turned choppy. Wind started to whip.

Bella flinched as she heard the sound of a helicopter approaching. Her ferryman glanced up and shook his head. "Not good weather to fly," he said. "Or to sail."

Anxiety mounted in Bella as the thudding of the chopper grew closer. If there was a gap in the blowing cloud they'd be sitting ducks—a red and a green light chugging across the dark water. Then she heard a second helicopter, the sound much fainter. Or was she imagining it?

The chopper came even closer, almost over them now. She gripped the side of the boat, knuckles white. But the helicopter was traveling fast and it went straight overhead, high above the cloud. Then she heard it heading away, up the coastline.

The sound of the second helicopter was also distant now, fading in the opposite direction. Bella allowed herself to take a shuddering breath.

A lighthouse on the mainland came into view, emitting a periodic pulse of weak light. As they entered a bay, the water grew calmer, and there was less mist.

She paid her fare, ran up the ramp. A cab was parked there, the driver inside sleeping. She rapped on the window. Startled by her appearance, he wound down the window just a crack.

"L'aéroport," she said breathlessly, rain plastering her hair to her face. *"Vite."* He asked which airport, she told him Charles de Gaulle.

She scrambled into the backseat, closed her eyes, prayed Hurley and Agnes were going to be okay. This was all her fault.

You came to wreck my life, profit from of my loss, my grief...

Bella started to shake hard. How many lives had been wrecked by this story—had Tariq been shot and killed up on that road because of her? Who'd been in the first car—MagMo and Etherington's men? Had they finally managed to assassinate the prince, finishing off what their bomb had failed to do at JFK? Had she led them right to his door?

Scoob's words ran through her mind.

If they got to them, made them talk, they're coming after you as we speak...

And they weren't going to stop with killing Tariq. They were going to keep coming after her until she was dead, too.

Tariq questioned the ferryman. The old islander was nervous, fidgeting, as he kept glancing at the one large bodyguard Tariq had brought with him down to the harbor.

Omair was back at the abbey with his own men, interrogating the injured MagMo operative they'd captured. A second operative had been killed. A third had been severely wounded in his shoulder by Tariq who had shot him as the man had tried to creep up the mountain from below. However, the wounded man had escaped with the aid of the fourth comrade, who'd managed to drag him back into the sedan and drive off as Tariq and his men had taken heavy fire from the helicopter above.

The chopper had pinned Tariq and his bodyguards in place for almost twenty minutes, before suddenly veering back up into the clouds, presumably to pick up the two escapees somewhere else on the island. Or because the pilot had detected Omair's helo coming in.

While the two MagMo operatives had escaped via chopper, the only way Bella could get off the island was by boat. The harbor was the first place they were looking for her now.

The ferryman explained that he thought the woman he'd given passage to might have been in trouble, but she'd told him that her mother was dying, that she needed desperately to fly home. She'd also paid cash, double the fare. He needed the money. His wife was not well.

Home, thought Tariq. Bella was going back to the States. She was going to break her story there. But if Sam Etherington used his apparent connections with STRIKE, Tariq figured that by the time Bella landed in the U.S., there'd be people waiting for her. And she wasn't going to make it.

"Was she injured?" he asked the ferryman.

"Just a mess. Her clothes were ripped, skin scratched. She said she'd fallen off her bicycle."

Relief rushed through Tariq's chest as he and his bodyguard returned to the bullet-ridden limo. From the car he called Omair. "The ferryman says he took her across to the mainland where she got a cab to the airport. We need to find out if she's at Orly or De Gaulle—I think she's going back to the States."

Forty minutes later their chopper had refueled and Tariq, Omair and several F.D.S. contract soldiers were in the air. Omair had contacted his Interpol connection in Paris and called in a favor.

The Interpol agent had managed to access the passenger manifests for flights departing for D.C. Bella DiCaprio had paid with credit card for a ticket on an Air France flight out of Charles de Gaulle.

Tariq was tense as they neared the airport, rubbing his crippled arm.

"You all right?" Omair said, watching his movements.

Tariq gave his brother a wry smile. "It's been good to use my body. I still have worth."

Omair's eyes were steady as he regarded his brother. "You could still work as a doctor, you know."

"Not a surgeon."

"Still."

"First," Tariq said quietly into his mouthpiece, "we take down The Moor, now that we think we know who he is."

"Or we leave him to the system."

Tariq shot his brother a sharp glance. "You getting soft, brother?"

Omair gave a dry laugh. "You're getting hard, Tariq." He was silent for a beat. "You were the one who said the cycle of violence must end here."

"We *can* use Bella," Tariq said. "If we get to her in time. We can work together."

"She must be something special for you to believe in her like this," Omair said.

Tariq looked out the window, at the lights below, approaching Paris, avoiding Omair's comment. He wasn't ready to articulate to his brother just what he felt for Bella right now. All he wanted was to find her safe.

Omair had handled the interrogation of their injured prisoner and their captive had let slip that the severely wounded escapee—the man Tariq had shot in the shoulder—was Amal Ghaffar.

This news had left Tariq and Omair cold.

Amal Ghaffar's father was the renowned billionaire industrialist Aban Ghaffar. Aban owned half of Manhattan and had helped steer and fund countless political campaigns. He also owned half of Dubai and had oil interests all over the Middle East. He was Arabic in origin and had been born in the Sahara.

"I'll bet Aban Ghaffar put money into Sam's campaign," Tariq said as he watched the lights below. "I can see Aban using this influence, along with Nikki's information, to blackmail Sam, to control the man most likely to take the most powerful office in the world come November. It would make Aban Ghaffar a quiet, global puppet master. And if in turn Sam used the U.S. military to back a MagMo-fuelled coup in our kingdom, supporting an alleged revolution for democracy, Aban would have our oil to use as a tool, too."

"Sam's not going to get into office, not now. Even if Bella never makes it back to the States, never manages to tell her story or use her proof, Nikki will come forward herself, and expose him. I'm impressed with Nikki—I never thought she'd do this. But she and Zakir agreed with you, Tariq. It all has to end here, even if it means reliving her past. We need a new era of peace, of safety for our families."

As the helo skids lightly touched ground at Charles de Gaulle, Omair said to Tariq, "I'm sorry for pushing you on this, for insisting I interrogate Bella."

Tariq gave a snort. "I don't think I've heard you apologize before."

Omair flashed a smile, teeth stark white against dark skin. "Not to you. But I can still hold it against you for allowing her to escape. That woman is determined."

"And strong," Tariq said, removing his headphones.

Then as the door was opened Omair added loudly above the sound of the rotors, "Faith says she will come forward, too. If you can find Bella, tell her she has our support, all of it. We will give her our full side of the story now!"

Tariq held his brother's gaze. "You have good women, both of you," he called out.

Omair grasped his shoulder. "Go find her! When Sam and Aban go down, we will all be safe again. Our country will be at peace. You and this reporter have made this possible now."

Tariq jumped down out of the chopper, moving quickly over the tarmac toward the waiting royal jet, two bodyguards flanking him. Behind him Omair and his men took off in the helo. They were going to search all hospitals, circling out from Ile-en-Mer. Amal Ghaffar had been gravely injured and would be in dire need of professional medical care. Omair was betting they'd find him in one of the emergency centers. But they needed to move fast before he was relocated to a private facility.

Because if they could get Amal, they would have further leverage against his father, Aban.

Minutes later Tariq's private jet taxied onto the runway. His pilot announced expected flight and arrival times—they would be at Dulles before Bella's commercial flight was due to land.

Tariq would be there first, waiting.

While Bella waited for her flight, she found an airport store where she bought a pair of jeans, T-shirt, a jacket and a pair of shoes. She also bought large sunglasses and a black ball cap. After she'd changed in the washroom and scrubbed her face, she put on the new shades and pulled the bill of the cap low over her brow. She then located a pay phone and called Mitchell Blake, her old editor at the *Washington Daily*.

Bella spoke fast, her gaze riveted on the flight board as she told Blake that she had irrefutable proof that Senator Sam Etherington and his aide, Isaiah Gold, had colluded with known terrorists to use a black ops U.S. hit squad in an attempt to assassinate Al Arif royalty. Then they'd had people murdered in an attempted cover-up. Hurriedly she outlined the basics of her story.

"I'm heading back to the States now. I'm going to break

this story on my Watchdog blog, but if I don't make it back, Blake, if something happens to me, follow this story up."

"Bella, are you—"

She hung up on him, hands shaking.

She'd omitted telling Blake that Sam Etherington's wife was still alive, and married to King Zakir. She was going to break this story without dragging Zakir's wife into it. For Tariq's sake. For her own sense of self-worth.

With trembling fingers Bella wiped tears out from under her dark glasses, thinking of the hatred and disgust she'd seen in Tariq's features as he'd looked down on her in the pool room and called her a muckraker, a bottom-feeder.

Now he was probably dead.

He'd never see that Bella DiCaprio had integrity.

She found and dialed the number for the FBI in D.C. She asked for the counterterrorism division.

Bella gave them her name, and informed them she had information that could threaten the security of the United States. She was transferred from one line to another and she imagined they were tracking her call, delaying her, recording the conversation. Checking her background. Whatever it was they did.

Her mouth went dry and her heart jackhammered as she waited. She shot another glance at the flight board— her plane had started boarding. Perspiration prickled over her lip.

Yet another agent came on the line, asking, again, the nature of her information and the threat. There was a crisp bite in his voice—they were taking her seriously now.

She rapidly outlined the details, yet again, and told them she had an audio recording that would prove Senator Sam Etherington's guilt.

There was a long beat of silence, but when the agent

spoke again, there was no change in his tone or tempo. "Do you have this proof on your person?"

"It's in a safe place in the States, and to access it I will need an FBI escort from Dulles International. My life is in danger."

"Can you tell us where this evidence is?"

"No, I can't."

"We'll need to bring you in," he said. "For questioning."

She gave them the number of her flight and arrival time. The agent said FBI agents would be waiting at Dulles when she landed.

As her plane lifted off, Bella prayed she hadn't made a mistake by contacting the FBI. But she was worried that her enemies might also be waiting. She needed protection to see this through to the end. Beyond exhausted, she fell into fitful sleep in her window seat, the seat beside her vacant. When she woke, they were still hours out from Dulles. She asked the flight attendant for some painkillers, pulled out her laptop and began to rough out her story—leaving Nikki out of it, leaving Tariq out of it. Focusing instead on STRIKE and Senator Sam Etherington. If she secured Scoob's audio, that was all the proof she would need. She'd beat the *Daily* to the story even though she'd tipped them off—there was no way they could get all this verified before she broke it on her blog. Once it had aired, the rest of the world could scramble after it, and run with it.

She typed furiously. Writing helped alleviate her worry over Hurley, Agnes, Scoob. It stopped her from hurting over Tariq.

But she couldn't erase from her mind that she'd brought danger—death—to his door.

Chapter 11

Jusef Al-Balawi pressed his balled-up shirt into Amal Ghaffar's wound. His friend's blood was warm on his fingers. In his other hand Jusef held a sat phone.

"He's dying," he yelled into the phone. "We need to take him to a hospital."

The voice that responded was like ice. "No hospital. If he dies, he dies. But I'm not going to risk an investigation and have him take my empire down. Refuel the helicopter, get back in the air, fly south, over the Spanish border. If you need to refuel again in Spain, do so, but no doctor. Once you've crossed the Mediterranean and entered Morocco, you can find medical attention there, someone who won't ask questions. Do not tell him who the patient is, or what happened."

Sweat pearled on Jusef's lip. "He won't make it that long."

"Look, you should have gone after the woman instead

of wasting time flying off the island with a dying man. And you should have killed the sheik. Instead you save this idiot, let them escape. You might have cost me everything!"

"This is your son you're talking about," Jusef said. "I believed *that* was important to you, to everything you stand for. *That* is why I made this decision."

"Your job is not to make decisions, or presumptions about me. Your job was to kill that woman before she destroys everything. The only thing I want is her dead." The phone went silent.

Jusef stared at the phone, something calcifying around his heart. He ordered the pilot to refuel the chopper. They were going to Spain.

In Manhattan Aban Ghaffar placed a call to Isaiah Gold. He was burning with fury over the fact he might lose his son. Over the fact he'd lost sight of Bella DiCaprio. That Tariq Al Arif was *still* alive.

"She got away," he said, very quietly, as soon as Isaiah answered. "I can't have her story getting out. You need to help me find her."

"I already have," Isaiah said.

Aban's grip tightened on his phone as his pulse quickened. "You're better than I thought, Mr. Gold. Where is she?"

"I was just about to call you," Isaiah said. "After she disappeared from the States we had her red-flagged in the system via Homeland Security in case she tried to reenter the country. Apparently she called the FBI from France, and when they ran her name though the database, our flag came up. The FBI agent called it in right away. My man in Homeland contacted me with the news."

Aban was silent. "Do the feds know what she's got?"

"They wouldn't divulge what she'd told them, but I fear it's serious—the agent who called it in is with the

FBI's counterterrorism division. They're meeting her at the Dulles International. Her Air France flight lands at 3:15 p.m. She'll be transported from there to the D.C. office."

Aban smoothed a hand over his steel-gray hair. "This information is invaluable, Mr. Gold, for both of us."

He hung up and immediately placed another call to one of his cell leaders in Washington.

"I have a job," he said quietly. "You need to move fast."

Tariq paced the arrivals area at Dulles International, watching the flight announcement board. Every now and then someone from the crowd would stare at him longer than was normal, and he'd remember his scarred face and clawed hand, his eye patch. He knew he must look frightening.

It cut him when a small child saw him and quickly grabbed his mother's hand, hiding behind her skirt. But otherwise he didn't think about it—he had no will to hide who he'd become. Not anymore.

Dr. Tariq Al Arif was back, fully, in the United States, and he didn't care who saw, or what the media wrote about him. He was focused only on finding Bella, making things right with her, letting her know his family would help her tell her story and drag Sam Etherington into the pit of hell.

This is my life, Tariq, my job...I have no one else.

His heart torqued. He knew now why she was insecure, why she had such a need to prove her worth. She didn't know where she'd come from, who her real parents were. That kind of thing could leave an insidious hole in the psyche, and Bella craved the one thing he had in abundance—blood family.

And he'd turned his back on them when he first moved

into the abbey. She'd helped him see it, and shown him the route home.

Now it was his turn to help her.

And he was going to show Bella she *did* have family she could turn to for help, protection, finances—*his*.

Suddenly he noticed what looked like federal agents moving rapidly through the gates of the arrival area. His gaze shot to the flight board.

Her plane had just landed.

Tariq and his two men scanned the rest of the hall, looking for anyone else suspicious also moving. But there was no threat he could identify. Unless the feds were a threat themselves. If Sam was powerful enough to have used STRIKE in an attempt to kill Omair and Faith, he could also be using feds, or at the very least, feeding them false information about Bella. He wondered how they'd come to be here—called by Bella herself? Or tipped off?

Tariq and his bodyguards tried to follow the agents as they moved rapidly through the sliding doors, but they were held back by security. Through the glass doors Tariq could see the agents—two women, three men—moving toward the docking chute. He imagined they were going to board the plane before anyone disembarked, escort her in.

Tension fisted in his gut. Time ticked by. He paced. Then the doors reopened, and he saw her.

His breath stopped.

She was handcuffed and arguing with one of the female agents.

They led her out through the sliding doors. Crowds of travelers parted, stopping to stare, whisper.

He ordered his men to stand down and he pushed through the crowd toward her. "Bella!"

She turned, froze.

"Tariq?" Her voice was hoarse, her eyes huge, dark purple pools, her face bloodless. She had scratches on her cheek.

The agents tried to usher her forward, but she fought them as she stared at him. "Oh, God," she said. "You're alive—I...I thought they shot you."

Tariq tried to go to her, to reach out for her. But one of the male agents slapped a hand on his arm, holding him back. Another agent's hand went for his sidearm.

"Why is she handcuffed?" Tariq demanded of the agent, motioning to his own men to stay back. "Is she under arrest?"

"Please, step aside, sir."

He held his ground.

"Is she under arrest?" he repeated. "If she's under arrest she has a right to a lawyer."

"Sir, I'm telling you to stand down, step back." The man's hand met the butt of the gun in his holster. The female agents started to lead Bella away.

"Tariq," she called out over her shoulder, tears suddenly sheening over her face. "I'll show you." Her voice cracked. "That I have integrity."

"Bella—"

But the agents ushered her forward and the crowd closed behind, swallowing them.

"Go get a vehicle!" he ordered his men.

Within minutes he had an airport limo and driver. He told the driver to take them to the FBI headquarters at the J. Edgar Hoover building on Pennsylvania Avenue. It was a gamble, but Tariq figured they'd take her there first. If not, he'd find out where they were holding her. While they drove, he called a top D.C. lawyer who had handled work for the Al Arifs before and told him to meet him at FBI headquarters.

Traffic was beginning to back up. People laid on horns. The driver's radio crackled.

"Congestion ahead," his driver told him. Then as they rounded a corner on an incline, Tariq could see the stream of cars stretching ahead of him. He sat forward suddenly as he noted three black Suburbans with tinted windows driving in convoy, heading the same direction he was. It had to be the feds, with Bella.

A chopper thudded somewhere in the air high above.

Perspiration broke out over his torso. "That motorcade down there, can you reach them?"

The driver glanced back over his shoulder. "Are you crazy, can you see this traffic? We're barely moving."

"Keep your eye on the convoy, try and get close." Tariq could feel it in his gut, it was them.

The traffic came to a snarling halt. Drivers started honking as a bus tried to budge into the stream. Tariq loosened the collar of his shirt. As long as he could see the motorcade, it was okay. Cars began to move again.

"Just stay on them," he demanded.

The driver chuckled. "You got a hidden camera in back there? We gonna be in the movies or something?"

Tariq didn't smile. His pulse was beginning to race—he had a bad feeling. He wound down his window, tried to see if he could spot the chopper. It gleamed high in the sky, and it was clearly hovering high over the stream of traffic. No markings on it that he could discern. Could be news chopper, doing traffic reports, weather. Could be anything.

He sat back, growing edgier as time ticked on and exhausts chugged fumes. The stream of vehicles began to move again. His men sat tense and silent at his side.

"Holy crap!" the driver said suddenly. "Do you guys see that?"

Tariq shot forward in his seat, peering through the windshield. Up ahead, a van had pulled into an intersection directly in front of the motorcade of Suburbans, cutting them off. Someone was emerging from the sunroof on top, his face obscured by a black balaclava—it looked like he was holding a shoulder rocket launcher!

Before Tariq could even register what was happening, the man fired his weapon. A flash of light, and the first Suburban blew into the air, smashing back against the one behind it, and landing on its side. Smoke began to billow black into the sky, tongues of orange flames licking up into it. Pedestrians were scattering. The assailant ducked back down into the van, and came up again. He fired again and this time his rocket exploded into the third SUV.

Ice coursed through Tariq's veins.

He flung open his door, began to run down the road, dodging in and out of cars, sweat dripping off him, his hip burning. His men raced after them. Tariq could hear screams. The chopper was lowering, bystanders now rushing forward to help. Smoke filled the air, black and acrid.

Tariq couldn't see what was happening with the attacker's van through the smoke—it was obscuring the intersection. He shoved a pedestrian aside as he jumped onto the sidewalk, then he heard a third rocket being discharged. Another explosion.

His mind screamed. He ran harder, sweat pouring off him.

Sirens were coming now, wailing in the distance.

He moved with singular focus, forcing his damaged leg to work, making his arm work, his lungs burning. As he made his way down the road through the lines of cars he could hear more screaming, yelling. He could smell the fire now, burning his nostrils.

In the road, one of the FBI agents was crawling away from the twisted metal of a burning SUV wreck. The second blast had missed the middle SUV in the motorcade and torn through the paving. But the force of the blast had thrown the vehicle up and onto its roof, and fire was licking out from under the engine. The sirens grew louder as ambulances and fire engines tried to come closer through the gridlock of cars.

Tariq scanned the scene. *Focus. Triage. Bella.* But his brain was looping back to that terrible day at JFK. He could hear the plane explosions going off in his head. Hear the same screaming, smell the scent of burning flesh, plane fuel strong in his nostrils. He was half blind, hot blood in his eye, looking for Julie. For a moment Tariq was frozen in a nightmare time warp. His bodyguard placed a hand on his arm. Tariq shook him off.

He *had* to move. He couldn't fail another woman he loved. Covering his mouth and nose with his jacket, he ran toward to upside-down SUV. "Help this man to the sidewalk!" he yelled, pointing at the federal agent trying to crawl clear of the fire. One of his men jumped to action, the other scanning the crowd, alert for changes.

Then Tariq saw her dark hair, pressed against the window of the vehicle. Tariq didn't think now, he just acted, adrenaline and instinct firing every molecule in his body. A young man was running forward with a fire extinguisher. He grabbed it from the man, and, using his good arm, smashed the window in front. Handing it back to the man, Tariq got on hands and knees, reached inside the vehicle. "Bella!"

But she was unresponsive. Flames were now licking into the inside of the vehicle from under the steering wheel. He had to make a decision. Fast. If she had a spinal injury he could paralyze or kill her if he tried to pull her out the window. But if he didn't drag her out and waited for the EMTs and firefighters to fight their way through the traffic and cut her free, there wouldn't be time before the entire car was engulfed in flames. She'd burn to death.

The flames were coming hot and fierce under the dash, crawling along a line of leaking fuel, even as the man sprayed the extinguisher on the engine.

"Help me!" he yelled to his bodyguard. *Don't fail. Not this time.*

And Tariq did it—with the help of his men he carefully began to edge and pull her out, fighting to make his lame hand move, thankful for having exercised it in the gym. Flames grew hotter, bigger. He could smell gas. Sweat dripped off his body.

"Hurry! It's going to blow!" the guy with the fire extinguisher yelled, stepping back as more fire burst out of the hood.

Tariq managed to pull Bella free. Together with his bodyguard, he carried Bella to the sidewalk. "There's another woman in the back of the car!" Tariq yelled, but as they set Bella down on the pavement, an explosion whooshed through the vehicle, swallowing it in fire.

A crowd formed around the pair.

"I'm a doctor, please, step back, give me some room." *I'm a doctor. I can do this. Focus.*

Her head was cut deeply. He could see bone. Her legs were at odd angles. Her pallor was gray. He prayed he hadn't furthered the damage by moving her, but if he'd left her in the car, she'd be burning to death right now.

Tariq felt for a pulse—she was alive. Breathing unobstructed, but unconscious and bleeding badly. He shucked his jacket and went into autopilot, stopping the most serious bleeding first with his bodyguard's help.

Sirens were everywhere now—law enforcement, firefighters, paramedics had arrived. People were being corralled, moved off scene, or into triage. EMTs pushed through the crowd to Bella. A military helicopter hovered ahead.

Within minutes the EMTs had her on a spine board.

Tariq ran after them and climbed into the ambulance behind her. "I'm family," he said urgently. "And a neurosurgeon. She's going to need surgery at once. Her head injury is bad. I have to be there when they operate."

He needed to make sure she had the best, and that he was at the surgeon's side in the operating room.

Tariq sat at Bella's bedside, holding her hand, monitoring her vitals. His men sat outside. Hospital machines clicked and wheezed and beeped—sounds of comfort to him. He hadn't slept in three days. But once again, even through this terrible tragedy, Bella had given him a gift—he'd been forced back into doctoring, into an operating room. He'd been coerced—in a way—to revisit that terrible bombing tragedy, and this time, he'd won. He was still Dr. Tariq Al Arif, and he *could* still make a difference.

He could still save lives.

Her surgeries had been difficult, but he'd been in there, instructing the surgeons. And she'd pulled through. This had shown him a way into the future, in his own profession. He could still teach. He could still help advise others. He could still do research. Bella had forced him to confront what in hindsight seemed to have been his biggest hurdle of all—where he'd failed Julie, it didn't mean he had to fail everyone else. And he *hadn't* failed Bella. She was his second chance—and he was not going to let her go.

She stirred, moaned, her eyelids blinking.

"Hey," he whispered, squeezing her hand. "I'm here. You're going to be okay."

Her eyelids fluttered open and Tariq's chest clutched at

the sight of those violet pools, those thick lashes, her gaunt cheeks, pale skin.

"Tariq?" Her voice came out hoarse. "You're still here?"

They'd removed the tubes only a few hours ago. He knew it had to hurt to speak.

"Shh, don't talk."

Her eyes widened suddenly. She tried to sit up. "How long have I been out?"

"No," he said, getting up, placing his hand on her shoulder. "You need to lie down, take it easy. Your legs are in braces—they had to put pins into one and a plate into the other."

Bella touched the bandage on her head, trying again to remember what happened.

She'd been in the FBI vehicle—that was the last thing she could recall. Then there'd been explosions. From that point she was missing a chunk of memory.

She frowned and it hurt. She tried to move her legs, but the braces held her still.

Her gaze went to the window that looked out into the hospital corridor. Two uniformed officers stood outside. Across from them sat two more men she recognized from the abbey.

"For your protection, mostly," Tariq said, following her gaze. "The feds are still waiting to talk to you."

"Scoob?" she said, struggling to sit up again. "I need to get—" Another piece of memory hit her. She reached for his arm. "Tariq—I saw you up on the road. The searchlight from the chopper lit you up, and there was a guy below you, with a gun."

"I got him first," he said quietly. "He escaped. But we know who he is. I have a lot to tell you, still."

She stared at him, emotion swelling into her chest, burning into her eyes. "I...I thought you were..." She sniffed back tears. "I thought I'd lost you."

"Never," he whispered.

"I wasn't going to tell Nikki's side of the story, Tariq. I was going to show you that I cared, that I had integrity, that my job wasn't all—"

"Bella, Nikki wants to come forward. She will tell you exactly what happened with Sam, how he tried to kill her. Faith will talk to you as well. She's Omair's partner, and she's the sniper that Travis Johnson sent to assassinate him."

Bella frowned, and it hurt. "Faith Sinclair? She was sent to kill Omair and...she's now his partner?"

"And they have a little son, Adam. It's a long, but interesting story. One you can use, if you want." Tariq smiled again, and Bella saw that crackle of energy in his eye that she'd once seen in a photo of him accepting a polo award. There was something new and vital about him. Or rather, a vibrant energy that had returned.

But Bella's brain was having trouble processing everything, and a wave of fatigue and nausea washed over her. She struggled to tamp it down.

"And you don't mind now, that people know you're alive? You're not hiding anymore."

He laughed, and the sound rippled warmly through her.

"No," he whispered, leaning forward as he cupped her face. "I want them to see me, and I want them to see my scars for what they are. You gave that to me. You brought me back from the edge of something so dark and terrible I didn't even notice it upon me."

He kissed her, his mouth lightly brushing her cracked lips. As he did, a male federal agent entered behind them, and coughed. A female agent entered at his side.

Tariq stood up, took Bella's hand in his, his gaze holding

hers. "There's nothing you need to hold back from them," he said quietly. "I've told them the royal family will cooperate fully in their investigation." He paused. "It's all going to come out, Bella, everything. And The Moor is going to go down. Thanks to you."

"You know who he is?"

He glanced at the agents. "We do. Like I said, we have much yet to talk about."

Two days later Bella was propped up in bed in a new private ward with her laptop and a phone. Tariq had taken care of everything financial, and he'd gotten her only the best of treatment and privacy. She was busy editing her story.

Her mother had flown in from Chicago and pretty much moved into Bella's hospital room. Minnie was fussing over the flowers, over the food, over Tariq, bossing hospital staff into place.

"Bella, my beautiful baby," she said, dark eyes luminous with emotion. "Why did you not tell me this was going on? Why did you not come to me?"

"What were you going to do, Mom, beat the bad guys off with a rolling pin?"

She clucked her tongue in mock disgust and stroked hair back from Bella's brow. "You know why I named you Bella." She glanced at Tariq. "It's because she's beautiful."

"I know she's beautiful."

"You will look after my baby."

"Mom," Bella growled, "Tariq has done everything he can."

She tutted.

Tariq took Minnie's arm. "Come, Mrs. DiCaprio, I'm going to buy you a coffee and a pastry downstairs. Bella has work to do."

"I don't drink coffee." Her hand went to her ample

bosom. "The doctor says it's not good for my heart. Now, my husband, you know, he drinks as much—"

Minnie's voice died as the door swung shut behind her and Tariq. Tariq grinned and gave Bella a wink through the glass as he marshaled Minnie off to the hospital cafeteria.

Bella smiled. She couldn't believe how much she loved this man. And she was going to do him proud. She got back to work quickly.

Already she'd had several calls from Mitchell at the *Daily*. They'd started digging into her tips, and combined with the attack on the FBI convoy, this news was busting wide open.

Other reporters and TV stations had called, too.

She'd told them nothing other than to check Watchdog for her blog post, which was going live before midnight tonight.

Meanwhile the feds were broadening their investigation and had taken the audio from the bank deposit box. They'd told her that Hurley's and Agnes's bodies had been found floating in the Potomac—they'd been tortured. Bella was now throwing her grief and remorse into the story. It was her retribution. Her revenge. She was doing it for them now.

For the underdog.

Scoob had come out of hiding, and he'd secretly let Bella listen to a copy of the audio he'd kept for himself and not told the feds about. She was using the details of that conversation between Isaiah Gold and Sam Etherington now, writing about how they'd conspired to order U.S. sniper Faith Sinclair to kill Omair. Both Faith and Nikki had spoken to her over the phone, giving their stories. Even King Zakir had given comment. It was mind-blowing content, the stuff of movies. How this family had defied death and found love even as an archenemy had hunted them down around the globe, and how their drama had found its way into the halls of the U.S. government.

And how it had all come into her own life.

Tears filled Bella's eyes as she typed. She was overwhelmed by the magnitude of it all, by how she'd personally been embraced by the powerful Al Arif clan. They'd taken her into their confidence, and they'd let her know they'd do everything they could to keep her safe. They made her feel wanted. And proud.

That night Bella clicked Publish. Her blog post went live.

The world was watching. The *Daily* had reporters on standby. Before 1:00 a.m. the next morning, it was on CNN, BBC, Sky News. All over the world the media was talking about the story. Pundits were scrambling to assess the impacts on U.S. foreign policy, the November presidential election. Stock markets went wild.

She'd beaten the FBI investigation to the punch, and Sam was arrested in front of hordes of cameras, the images of his humiliation being beamed live by satellite into the homes of people glued to televisions around the globe. Isaiah Gold was arrested simultaneously in the same ignoble fashion.

And so was Amal Ghaffar.

Her hospital phone began to ring.

Tariq was at her side now, and he reached for the phone.

"No," she said. "I don't want to talk to anyone, not yet."

He pulled the plug, held it up and smiled. "You did it, Bella. You took them down."

"We did it." She paused. "What did you do with my mother, by the way? Has she gone home? Things are suddenly...so peaceful."

He grinned. "That's my secret."

"She likes you."

His features turned serious. "I like her. She raised you, Bella. Believe it or not, I can see a lot of you in Minnie DiCaprio."

Bella bit her lip, nodded. "I do love her. I love them all. I…I should have gone home to see them more often. I should have been there for them, too. That's going to change." She hesitated. "Thank you, Tariq."

"For?"

"For making me see I do have family. The rest is not important."

"It is important," he said, "to know where you came from. But it's mitigated, Bella, by the love you do have around you."

"I know."

She thought of her friends, too, of Hurley and Agnes. And she wished they were alive to see that Watchdog had gone viral. They'd brought Bella over to the "dark side" and she'd managed to shine the light of the media world on them. The victory was bittersweet.

"Hey," Tariq said, taking her hand, seemingly reading her mind. "There was nothing you could have done to stop it."

She bit her lip, nodded. "I hope the people responsible burn in hell," she said.

"They will."

Bella looked up into his scarred face, his arrogant, aristocratic features, and she inhaled deeply. "I wanted to say, in the pool room that night, that I loved you before I ever got to Ile-en-Mer. I want you to understand, Tariq, that I always cared." She swallowed against the emotion balling in her throat. "I never came to hurt you."

"I know that," he said. "I went and read every one of the articles you ever wrote about me and my family, and I came to that realization. It made me believe you would co-operate with us, and leave Nikki out after I told you what she'd been through. I wanted us to work together, and I fought with my own brothers over it. But before I could tell you any of this, you were gone."

Tears flooded her eyes.

He took her face in his hands. "Listen to me—I've rented a brownstone here in Washington. There's lots of room, even a place for your mother. That's where she is now, doing some redecorating, I suspect. And I've hired staff to take care of you while you can't get around. I want you to live there with me, Bella, until you're properly back on your feet. And in the meantime I plan on convincing you that we belong together for a lot longer than just your rehabilitation." He paused, his gaze piercing hers. "I am going to show you just how much you are worth. To me. To my family."

"Tariq." Her voice caught. "You're messing with me—because this sounds an awful lot like a proposal."

"It is."

Words died on her lips. She stared at him. His features were dead serious.

Then slowly, quietly, she said, "It's too soon, Tariq. You've been through too much. I don't believe you've fully grieved."

"I need you, Bella. I need you at my side."

"What about the abbey? What about—"

"I've had some time to think. I'm going to donate the estate to the opera foundation on Ile-en-Mer. They can use it for whatever they want, hotel, performances, they can give ghost tours, exhume the abbess's bones, bury her properly in the cemetery. Bring closure."

The tears slid down Bella's face, and her heart ached with so much love she thought she might die.

"Say something," he said.

But she was shaking like a leaf, choking with emotion, and she could only nod.

He gathered her tightly into his arms and kissed her hard on the mouth. Powerful, dominant. Sure.

Tariq had never been more certain of anything—this woman was the best thing that had happened in his life. She had a vitality and passion that made him whole. But it had been one hell of a ride to get here. And he was not going to let her go. She was his second chance—he was going to show her it was worth it.

* * * * *

Look for Dalilah's story,
GUARDING THE PRINCESS,
the next exciting chapter of Loreth Anne White's
new miniseries, SAHARA KINGS.
Available January 2013,
wherever Harlequin books are sold.

COMING NEXT MONTH from Harlequin®
Romantic Suspense
AVAILABLE SEPTEMBER 18, 2012

#1723 THE COWBOY'S CLAIM
Cowboy Café
Carla Cassidy
When Nick's secret son is kidnapped, he and Courtney, the woman he left behind, must work together to save him.

#1724 COLTON'S RANCH REFUGE
The Coltons of Eden Falls
Beth Cornelison
Movie star Violet Chastain witnesses an Amish girl's kidnapping, so grumpy ex-soldier Gunnar Colton is assigned to protect her—and babysit her rambunctious toddler twins.

#1725 CAVANAUGH'S SURRENDER
Cavanaugh Justice
Marie Ferrarella
A woman finds her sister dead and goes on a rampage to find out the truth, running headlong into romance with the investigating detective.

#1726 FLASH OF DEATH
Code X
Cindy Dees
With a dangerous drug cartel out to kill them both, can wild child Trent break through the cold, cautious shell Chloe has erected and find love?

You can find more information on upcoming Harlequin® titles, free excerpts and more at www.Harlequin.com.

HRSCNM0912

REQUEST YOUR FREE BOOKS!
2 FREE NOVELS PLUS 2 FREE GIFTS!

ROMANTIC
SUSPENSE

Sparked by Danger, Fueled by Passion.

YES! Please send me 2 FREE Harlequin® Romantic Suspense novels and my 2 FREE gifts (gifts are worth about $10). After receiving them, if I don't wish to receive any more books, I can return the shipping statement marked "cancel." If I don't cancel, I will receive 4 brand-new novels every month and be billed just $4.49 per book in the U.S. or $5.24 per book in Canada. That's a saving of at least 14% off the cover price! It's quite a bargain! Shipping and handling is just 50¢ per book in the U.S. and 75¢ per book in Canada.* I understand that accepting the 2 free books and gifts places me under no obligation to buy anything. I can always return a shipment and cancel at any time. Even if I never buy another book, the two free books and gifts are mine to keep forever.

240/340 HDN FEFR

Name	(PLEASE PRINT)
Address	Apt. #
City	State/Prov.	Zip/Postal Code

Signature (if under 18, a parent or guardian must sign)

Mail to the **Reader Service:**
IN U.S.A.: P.O. Box 1867, Buffalo, NY 14240-1867
IN CANADA: P.O. Box 609, Fort Erie, Ontario L2A 5X3

Not valid for current subscribers to Harlequin Romantic Suspense books.

Want to try two free books from another line?
Call 1-800-873-8635 or visit www.ReaderService.com.

* Terms and prices subject to change without notice. Prices do not include applicable taxes. Sales tax applicable in N.Y. Canadian residents will be charged applicable taxes. Offer not valid in Quebec. This offer is limited to one order per household. All orders subject to credit approval. Credit or debit balances in a customer's account(s) may be offset by any other outstanding balance owed by or to the customer. Please allow 4 to 6 weeks for delivery. Offer available while quantities last.

Your Privacy—The Reader Service is committed to protecting your privacy. Our Privacy Policy is available online at www.ReaderService.com or upon request from the Reader Service.

We make a portion of our mailing list available to reputable third parties that offer products we believe may interest you. If you prefer that we not exchange your name with third parties, or if you wish to clarify or modify your communication preferences, please visit us at www.ReaderService.com/consumerchoice or write to us at Reader Service Preference Service, P.O. Box 9062, Buffalo, NY 14269. Include your complete name and address.

HRS11B

HARLEQUIN®

SPECIAL EDITION

Life, Love and Family

Sometimes love strikes in the most unexpected circumstances...

Soon-to-be single mom Antonia Wright isn't looking for romance, especially from a cowboy. But when rancher and single father Clayton Traub rents a room at Antonia's boardinghouse, Wright's Way, she isn't prepared for the attraction that instantly sizzles between them or the pain she sees in his big brown eyes. Can Clay and Antonia trust their hearts and build the family they've always dreamed of?

Don't miss

THE MAVERICK'S READY-MADE FAMILY

by Brenda Harlen

Montana ★MAVERICKS
BACK IN THE SADDLE

Available this October from Harlequin® Special Edition®

HSE65697

Out of the corner of her eye, she saw that the SUV was empty. Past it, near the trailhead, she glimpsed the beam of a flashlight bobbing as it headed down the trail.

The trail was wide and paved, and she found, once her eyes adjusted, that she didn't need to use her flashlight if she was careful. Enough starlight bled down through the pine boughs that she could see far enough ahead—she also knew the trail well.

There was no sign of Jordan, though. She'd reached the creek and bridge, quickly crossed it, and had started up the winding trail when she caught a glimpse of light above her on the trail.

She stopped to listen, afraid he might have heard her behind him. But there was only the sound of the creek and moan of the pines in the breeze. Somewhere in the distance, an owl hooted. She moved again, hurrying now.

Once the trail topped out, she should be able to see Jordan's light ahead of her, though she couldn't imagine what he was doing hiking to the falls tonight.

There was always a good chance of running into a moose or a wolf or, worse, this time of a year, a hungry grizzly foraging for food before hibernation.

The trail topped out. She stopped to catch her breath and listen for Jordan. Ahead she could make out the solid rock area at the base of the falls. A few more steps and she could feel the mist coming off the cascading water. From here, the trail carved a crooked path up through the pines to the top of the falls.

There was no sign of any light ahead and the only thing she could hear was the falls. Where was Jordan? She rushed on, convinced he was still ahead of her. Something rustled in the trees off to her right. A limb cracked somewhere ahead in the pines.

She stopped and drew her weapon. Someone was out there.

The report of the rifle shot felt so close it made the hair stand up on her neck. The sound ricocheted off the rock cliff and reverberated through her. Liza dived to the ground. A second shot echoed through the trees.

Weapon still drawn, she scrambled up the hill and almost tripped over the body Jordan Cardwell was standing over.

What was Jordan doing up at the falls so late at night? And is he guilty of more than just a walk in the moonlight?

Find out in the highly anticipated sequel
JUSTICE AT CARWELL RANCH
by USA TODAY *bestselling author*
B.J. Daniels.

Catch the thrill October 2, 2012.